A Special Delivery

Patsy stopped at the street corner. She had been holding the new secret long enough. "We aren't far from the State House," she said.

Barbara said, "I know that. What does it matter?"

"I think we should go. As Daughters of Liberty."

"What are you saying? You make no sense. The Congress is meeting. They won't have two girls hanging about."

Patsy could barely keep the excitement from her voice. "I found a note! In the man's haversack. When he fell from the horse, his sack popped open and I found a note. It seems to be of true importance, Barb. I had just a second to look at it, but I recognized the words *army* and *river*. Let's read it. See if we don't think it is something the Daughters of Liberty should take to the Congress at the State House."

Patsy flattened the note. She was surprised to find her fingers trembling a bit. Was this truly something of importance?

Daughters of Liberty

Available from MINSTREL Books

DAUGHTERS *of* LIBERTY

PATSY'S DISCOVERY

Elizabeth Massie

A MINSTREL® BOOK

Published by POCKET BOOKS

New York   London   Toronto   Sydney   Tokyo   Singapore

A MINSTREL PAPERBACK *Original*

A Minstrel Book published by
POCKET BOOKS, a division of Simon & Schuster Inc.
1230 Avenue of the Americas, New York, NY 10020

Copyright © 1997 by Elizabeth Massie

ISBN: 0-671-00132-9

First Minstrel Books printing July 1997

10 9 8 7 6 5 4 3 2

A MINSTREL BOOK and colophon are registered trademarks of Simon & Schuster Inc.

Cover art by Ernie Norcia

Printed in the U.S.A.

To my daughter, Erin Christine Massie.
Find your dream; do what makes your heart sing!

1

"Shhh, be quiet now or we'll both be in trouble! How did you get out of the stable in the first place?"

Twelve-year-old Patsy Black leaned out the open window in the tavern's back bedroom, scolding the little black and white puppy in the garden. He sat in a spot of early morning sunlight, wagging his tail and looking very pleased with himself. His nose and fur were flecked with soil. Not far from the dog was one of Mother's favorite rosebushes, and beneath the bush, a large hole with a soft mound of dirt by it. If Patsy's father saw the puppy and the hole he had dug, he would have a stern word with Patsy and would send the dog away for good.

"You know you shouldn't be in the garden. Father will catch you and send you off if he sees you," Patsy said, pushing a loose strand of blond hair back beneath her plain white mobcap. "You do want to live here at Black's Tavern, don't you?"

The puppy wagged his black and white tail so hard that his body nearly tipped over. He barked once. It looked as though he was smiling.

"Oh, do be quiet!" Patsy quickly put her needlepoint sampler on the dresser, held her skirt and petticoat carefully, and climbed out through the window. The corner of her apron caught on a holly branch and was twisted askew as she dropped onto the soft ground of the garden. She tugged the apron to pull it straight and heard it rip. "Not again!" she said. She would have to sew it up so Mother wouldn't notice. A girl wasn't supposed to be clambering in and out windows.

Oh, why can't girls dress in trousers like boys? Patsy thought. *It would be so much easier to go places.*

The puppy barked again, thrilled to have someone in the garden to play with him.

"Oh, not now we won't!" Patsy exclaimed. She grabbed the puppy and hurried along the brick

walkway among the roses, trimmed hedges, black-
berry bushes, and lilacs to the garden gate. "I'll
fill that hole back in as soon as I have you where
you belong," she told the dog. "And somehow I
must teach you not to dig. You are as bad as my
little brother, Nicholas."

The puppy wriggled, trying to get down, but
Patsy only held on more tightly.

The previous week, Patsy's father, Andrew
Black, had made his opinion on puppies very
clear. "Dogs are only good to have around a stable," he had said when Patsy asked if she could
keep the puppy. "They eat rats and mice and
other vermin. But a dog for a pet is frivolous,
Patsy. We cannot afford such a waste of money
and a waste of time."

"He hasn't any other home, Father," Patsy had
pleaded. "He was so sad when I found him, shiv-
ering and whining across the road, all alone and
abandoned. He shall surely starve or become
mean and wild if we do not take care of him."

Mr. Black had stood in the foyer of Black's
Tavern, adjusting his tricornered hat and drawing
on his riding gloves. "Dear daughter," he had
said, "you have duties here. I have duties, and so

★ 3 ★

does your mother. We haven't time to care for a mutt."

It was then that Patsy had thought of Barbara Layman. She was Patsy's best friend and lived with her family above Black's Stable. Barbara loved animals. "What if I give him to Barbara?" Patsy had asked. "Then he can live in the stable and I can play with him there. He can catch rats and earn his keep. Please, Father?"

Mr. Black had taken a deep breath, tugged on the heavy front door, and walked out to the marble stoop. Patsy had followed, drawing her shawl around her shoulders against the cool air of the May morning. Out on Philadelphia's Mulberry Street, the day was already bustling. Dust rose into the air with the pounding of horses' hooves and the rattling of carriage wheels. Mr. Black's gray horse, Thunder, was saddled and tethered to one of the posts in front of Black's Tavern. Mr. Black pulled the reins free, gathered them up, and mounted. Then he looked down at his daughter. His face had softened.

"Very well, Patsy," he'd said. "We'll give it a try. But the dog lives at the stable. You will play with him there when your chores are done. I do not want to see him hanging about the tavern grounds getting underfoot of our customers. Promise me that."

"I promise!"

And a week later, for the third time since Patsy's promise, the puppy had found his way into the side garden. And for the third time he had dug a hole beneath the rosebushes.

Patsy pushed open the low picket gate. She didn't have to latch it back, because there was a chain with an iron ball that was connected at one end to a post. The chain stretched out as the gate was opened, then, with the weight of the ball, was pulled back into place. It was certainly heavy enough to keep a puppy from pushing it open. But to the side of the gate was a mound of dirt and a hole. He'd dug his way under.

"Gracious!" said Patsy to the puppy. "I should have you apprenticed to a well-digger. Such talent is wasted on our poor tavern property."

Down the dirt path Patsy went, along Mrs. Brubaker's vast stone wall to her left, past the tavern's hooded well and patch of apple trees. She went by the smokehouse, tipping her head back to take in the wonderful salty scents of ham and curing beef.

Black's Stable was at the end of the path, surrounded by its own whitewashed fencing. There was a small grassy paddock, a blacksmith's shop, and then the ten-stalled stable in which the visitors to the tavern paid seven pence to board their horses during their stay.

The stable was two stories high; on the second floor, the Layman family kept house. Mr. Layman managed the stable and cared for the horses. Mrs. Layman worked at Boxler's Milliner on High Street. Barbara Layman, Patsy's best friend, helped her father during the day and her mother during the evenings.

"Good morning, Miss Black!" called a voice from inside the blacksmith's shop.

Patsy peeked in through the open door. Inside was a bright orange glare and the whooshing sound of the bellows. Mr. Norris, the blacksmith, was hunched over his anvil, holding a red-hot spike with a vise and pounding it flat with a hammer. His apprentice, Randolph Bonner, was regulating the fire in the forge with air pumped from the bellows. Both men wore scuffed, buckled shoes, stained breeches, and leather aprons. It was too hot in the little workshop for the men to wear shirts. Most blacksmiths in Philadelphia had their own businesses, working independently, but Patsy's father had enough business to make a black-smith on the grounds a profitable enterprise. Mr. Norris made nails and iron tools for building repairs. And if a visitor's horse needed a shoe, he could do that, too. There had been some men in town who had tried to recruit Mr. Norris into making tools for the soldiers of King George, but Mr. Norris refused. He never said it out loud, but Patsy knew the man was a patriot. It was the year 1776, and the colonies had already been in battles with the soldiers of the Crown. Mr. Norris wanted independence for the colonies. He was a young man, always kind and happy to take a moment from his work to speak to Patsy.

"Good morning!" Patsy called over the ping of metal against metal.

Mr. Norris smiled. His face was covered with streaks of soot. "I see you are about early today," he said. "How is your puppy?"

The puppy was squirming in Patsy's hands, and it was all she could do to keep from losing her grip. "He's well, Mr. Norris," said Patsy. "And lively, as you can see. But he can't seem to learn that he must stay back at the stable, lest he get himself and me into serious trouble."

Putting the vise down and wiping one hand with

his other, gloved hand, Mr. Norris smiled. "Have you come up with a name for the pup yet? When I asked you several days ago, you said you had yet to find one to suit his personality."

"Not yet, sir," Patsy said. "My mother suggested Spot or Yips, for the way he barks in such a short little voice. But neither one seems right. I just have to wait until I can think of the best name."

"Until then," asked Mr. Norris, "how do you call him?"

Patsy scratched the puppy behind his ears. "I say, 'Come here!' "

Mr. Norris chuckled. Then he turned back to his work, lifting the vise, gripping the cooling iron, and dipping it into a bucket of water, where it sizzled and a puff of steam rose into the air.

"Patsy!"

Patsy turned in the direction of the voice. Standing just inside the stable's sunny paddock and holding a large basket of potatoes was Barbara Layman. She was a pretty girl, just a year older than Patsy, with black curly hair and hazel eyes. Her dress was a sunny yellow.

Clutching the puppy tightly, Patsy skipped down the path and stopped at the paddock fence.

Barbara furrowed her brows, though her mouth retained its usual fun-filled smile. "Did that mutt get into your garden again?"

"Yes," said Patsy. "And dug another hole under one of Mother's rosebushes. He's going to be sent away if he doesn't stay back here at the stable where he belongs." She put the puppy down, and he bounded to Barbara, who rested her basket on the ground and gave the puppy a hearty scratching behind his ears.

"I'm sorry," Barbara said. "He stayed in the stable all night, sleeping in the stall with my pony. I didn't know he'd gone up the path to the garden while I was collecting potatoes this morning."

Patsy said, "He hasn't learned yet to stay put. I think you should tie him up if you are going to leave him alone."

"Tie him up?" Barbara shook her head. "What fun is it for a dog to be tied up?"

"I worry more about him getting into the side garden than I do him having fun. What fun would he have if Father sent him off to the streets? He would be trampled by a carriage or one of those careless boys who race their horses so fast down our lane. He would be kicked and pushed about, and maybe even starve to death!"

Barbara shook her head in good humor. "Enough, Patsy! I can see your point. I'll make sure the puppy stays here at the stable."

Suddenly a tall, smiling man with thinning hair and shirt sleeves rolled up poked his head out the stable door and said, "Hello, Patsy Black. And how is your family this morning?"

"Fine, Mr. Layman," Patsy called back.

"And are you done with your chores for the morning?" he asked. "Barb has more to do before she can play."

Patsy shook her head. "No, sir. I just had something to," she hesitated, "something to deliver to Barb."

The puppy, on the ground, snapped at a hopping cricket and barked.

"Delivering that dog again," said Mr. Layman. He chuckled. "Shall we ever train that dog to be a proper stable animal? He has yet to catch a mouse or chase away prowlers. He only chews on the hoof trimmings the farrier leaves behind."

Patsy grimaced. "That's foul!"

Mr. Layman and Barbara both laughed. "Foul but true," said Barbara. "You are such a city girl!"

Patsy nodded. They were right. Patsy had

grown up here in Black's Tavern. She knew more about polishing silver and pewter than she did taking care of animals. Barbara Layman's family, however, had moved from the country to the city only three years ago. Barbara knew all about caring for pigs, cows, horses, and goats. She also was handy in her family's vegetable plot behind the stable.

"Take those potatoes upstairs," Mr. Layman said to his daughter. "And then curry the sorrel in the last stall. His master is leaving this morning. Patsy, good day to you."

Patsy gave a little curtsy to the Laymans and a stern look to the spotted puppy, and ran back to the tavern. She crept in through the bedroom window and picked up her stitching just in time.

The narrow bedroom door swung open, and Mrs. Black came in with several woolen blankets over her arm.

"How is the sampler coming, Patsy?" she asked.

"Fine," Patsy said to her mother. Holding the needle, she could see that her fingers were now filthy from carrying the dog. There was a smudge of dirt on the white cloth she was embroidering.

And there was the new tear in her apron. *Oh, dear!* she thought. She put one hand over the tear.

"I'll check it over when I get a free moment," said Mrs. Black. "But I've got a customer upstairs who is still asleep. A Mr. Francis, who told everyone within earshot last evening that he had urgent business this morning. It's nearly eight-thirty. I think he would appreciate being awakened."

Patsy shook her head. "You are mother to them all, just like Father says. You see these men, old and young, as just more children to tend and care for."

Rebecca Black smiled. A short woman with brown hair and green eyes, she had more energy than anyone Patsy ever knew. More than Mr. Norris, more than Patsy's brothers, Nicholas and Henry. And she was quick and clever. Often Mrs. Black would banter with the men who stayed at the tavern and leave them wondering at her wisdom.

"I suppose that's true," Mrs. Black answered. "And that may well be why our tavern is one of the most popular in all of Philadelphia. Not only do the men get room and board, they get someone to wake them and darn their socks and give them tonic when they've had too much to eat.

Now, back to your sampler, dear. And watch the clock. At nine, turn your needle to mending the holes in these blankets. The men's toes go straight through sometimes, and if we don't catch the holes quickly, they'll turn into tears. After that, check the supply of candles in the guest rooms."

"Yes, ma'am," said Patsy. Then she asked the question she'd been asking her mother every day for the past week. "How are you feeling, Mother? Are you well?"

Mrs. Black nodded. In just two months she was going to have a new baby. This didn't slow her down, however. Even though she no longer did heavy work, she was up and about, directing her children and the hired help with her usual enthusiasm. Patsy hoped the new baby would be a girl to even it out with the two boys in the family.

"Women have been having babies ever since the world was created," said Mrs. Black. "We must trust the Lord to take care of us. And Katherine Ralston has fine midwifing skills. Don't worry." Then Mrs. Black left the bedroom, pulling the door shut.

Patsy knew her mother was right. Katherine had delivered many babies. There was little about which to worry.

Dipping her hands into the bowl of water on the dresser, Patsy wiped them off on her apron. She glanced at the dirty sampler, then quickly dipped it in the bowl, too. But the dirt spot merely became a mud spot. She put the ball of soap to it and rubbed hard. Finally it was clean and white again.

Settling into the straight-backed chair, Patsy carefully worked three more letters into the wet cloth. Then she held it up. It looked just fine. She would have it done in just a few days. Mother would be proud and would stretch it on a frame to hang beside the sampler she had done as a girl, so long ago. She lay the sampler on the windowsill where the sun could dry it quickly.

Patsy rummaged through the dresser drawer and found a spool of heavier thread. She moved to the bed. Wiggling around, she tried to loosen the bony stays at her waist, pushed her shoes off, then drew her stockinged feet up under her and leaned against the down-filled pillow. The light wasn't as good as it was by the chair, but the bed was more comfortable. First she mended her apron. Then she took the needle to the blankets.

In this small bedroom, Patsy's entire family slept at night. The bed on which Patsy sat was where her father and mother slept. There was another bed next to it on which sixteen-year-old Henry and seven-year-old Nicholas slept. Patsy had a trundle bed which stayed beneath her parents' bed during the day and then was pulled out at night. Sometimes Nicholas laughed, saying Patsy had to sleep in a "little girl's bed," but Patsy didn't care. At night, close to the floor, she felt safe and secure. And besides, she didn't have anyone trying to take all the covers and kicking her. Sometimes in the dark she would hear Nicholas and Henry arguing in whispers about the other taking up too much space.

When the mending was complete, she went out of the bedroom and into the Red Horse Room, where men played cards and smoked in the evenings. It was midmorning, so most of the tavern visitors were out about their business. Only one old man sat in a window seat, puffing on his clay pipe and staring out the window at the traffic on the street. On the table at his elbow was paper and pen, and on the paper some sketches of faces.

"Good morning, sir," Patsy greeted him with a small curtsy.

He glanced over at her and nodded silently, then looked back out the window.

"I see you are an artist?"

The man looked down at the paper, then up at Patsy. "Of a sort, young lady. I like to dabble in that which interests me." Then he looked back out the window.

"Good morning," Patsy excused herself. She walked through the Red Horse Room and into the foyer. She paused for a moment to look into the Ulysses Room, where the men dined on tasty hot meals. There were many tables, room enough for forty to dine at once. The floor was bright polished oak. The wooden venetian blinds on the tall windows were open, letting in the sunlight. Once a week, Black's Tavern would host a dance, and the place would swarm with gaily dressed folks. Tables would be moved and chairs would be lined along the walls. A small ensemble of musicians, usually a harpsichord, a violin, and a recorder, would play in one corner while the men and women danced. With rare exceptions, dances were the only times women, besides the Blacks, were allowed in the tavern. Men, everyone knew, wanted and demanded their privacy.

"If you have time for woolgathering," called the man from the Red Horse Room, "then perhaps once you put those blankets away you could find a spare minute to bring me a new pouch of tobacco."

Patsy said, "Yes, sir. Right away." She went into the pantry at the end of the hall and collected a pouch of tobacco. Then she took it back to the man, who nodded without looking at her and began to press the dried leaves into the bowl of his pipe. Patsy skipped up the stairs with the blankets.

Black's Tavern was not the largest tavern in the city, but it was very popular. It had five bedrooms upstairs. Each room had two or three beds in which up to five men could sleep at once. The beds were fine, with flock-filled mattresses and pillows. Heavy, good quality bed hangings were tied back to the posters, ready to be loosened and drawn around on a cold evening. Soon, in June, Patsy and her mother would replace the heavy hangings with ones of lighter fabric, which would allow air to circulate but would keep flying insects out of the men's faces as they slept.

For the men who came to the tavern, a sleeping space was first come, first served. The first to arrive would get their choice of room and bed; those who came later would have to take what was left. On especially busy evenings there might not be enough beds for men, and some would have to sleep on the floor in front of the fireplaces. There were few complaints. The tavern had cozy fireplaces indeed.

The mended blankets went on a chest in the first room. Then Patsy checked all the candlesticks and found only three burned down beyond use. She pulled out the stubs, which would be melted down again.

She paused at the top of the stairs, looking out the window at the side garden and the stone wall that separated the property of Black's Tavern from the property of Mrs. Josiah Brubaker. Last year there had been a white picket fence bordering the two properties. But in the summer Mrs. Brubaker decided a fence wasn't enough to ensure her privacy. She swore to Mr. Black that Patsy's little brother, Nicholas, was trying to spy on her through the fence slats. Of course, Nicholas *was* trying to spy. Any boy would have curiosity about such a mean old woman. But he would never admit it. And so Mrs. Brubaker had had the wall built. Even though it was usually just public buildings that had such walls, with homes and businesses delineated by graceful fences, Mrs. Brubaker was determined and got her way. The wall was four and a half feet tall, of solid gray stone. But it only proved to Patsy once more that Mrs. Brubaker was a shrew, a mean old woman who could find a reason to argue over anything.

From the window upstairs, Patsy could see into Mrs. Brubaker's garden. It was beautiful, but like a set of china, never used. There were brick walkways winding through boxwood hedges and geometric plots of flowers and vegetables. Several wooden benches sat along the open walk, with another bench beneath the ivy-covered trellis in the garden's center.

No one ever enjoys that garden, Patsy thought. *Mrs. Brubaker is a widow and has no children. It would be such a fine garden for children.*

Mrs. Brubaker's husband had died a long time ago, before Patsy was born. He had left his wife enough money to run her household and employ a gardener, but that was about all Patsy knew about her neighbor. However, Patsy did know enough to stay out of the woman's way if ever they met on the street. She was sharp-tongued and impatient. A cheery smile and a pleasant greeting could not melt the woman's constant frown.

Even Mr. and Mrs. Black knew it was best to leave Mrs. Brubaker alone.

2

Patsy noticed the candle stubs in her hands and wondered how long she had been staring out the window. Quickly she went downstairs, through the hall, and out into the backyard.

There was bustling activity in the yard behind the tavern. The Black family had hired several people to help run the business of the tavern. Two were older spinster Quaker women, twin sisters, Molly and Martha Anderson. They worked to bring money in to their parents and were plain, somber women who made candles, cooked, and helped with other odd jobs as needed. Then there was Katherine Ralston, a lively young lady in her twenties who cleaned, cooked, churned, and took such a kind interest in Patsy that it was as though she were an older sister rather than a servant.

This morning the Andersons were preparing a big kettle for candle making. Although there were shops in town that would sell candles to the tavern, Mr. Black took pride in being as self-sufficient as possible, and that went as far as taking care of his own supply of candles. Besides, he always said the beeswax candles made in the backyard were far superior to any for which he might lay out a shilling.

Patsy dropped the candle stubs into the kettle of melting wax. Wicks were already strung through the wooden rods, ready to be dipped. It took at least twenty good dips to make a beeswax candle.

"Are thou here to help us?" asked Martha Anderson.

"Oh," said Patsy. She had liked making candles when she was smaller. But it grew tedious very fast, and she much preferred to help Katherine when the chance came. "I'm not certain. Let me check with my mother to see what she would have me do."

Patsy hurried to the kitchen, which was a small building separate from the tavern in order to prevent smells and heat from affecting the main building. Inside, Mrs. Black was instructing Katherine on the afternoon meal, which was held at four o'clock sharp. Katherine gave Patsy a wink as she entered.

"Mother, may I help Katherine with meal preparations? I do so think I have a lot to learn yet about cooking."

"My dear, certainly," said Mrs. Black. "You are making breads and soups today, and there are fresh oysters as well. Mind you listen to Katherine."

"I will," said Patsy.

Mrs. Black left the kitchen. Patsy watched her as she crossed by the Andersons, spoke briefly, then went inside the tavern.

"So what chore are you trading for cooking?" asked Katherine with a knowing smile. She was a pretty woman with reddish hair and blue eyes. She was engaged to a man who was an apprentice to a bookbinder, and she hoped to be married when his apprenticeship was up and he had earned the status of journeyman. "I don't ever remember you being enthusiastic for chopping vegetables or rolling dough. What are you avoiding? Candle making?"

"Yes," said Patsy, wrinkling her nose.

"That isn't a hard job," said Katherine.

"Indeed not. But to stand there for any time with the two of them makes me feel itchy for wanting to tell a joke or even smile a bit. They are so somber I'd just about fall asleep on my feet being around them."

Katherine laughed out loud. "Well said. I try my hardest to cheer them, but they are apt and determined to keep the corners of their mouths from turning up even the slightest. Maybe if we stood them on their heads we could pass their expressions for smiles?"

Working with Katherine was a pleasure. The two of them chopped carrots and potatoes and onions from the tavern garden and put them in with chicken stock. The kitchen fireplace was large enough for several dishes to be cooking at once. To the side of the fireplace was a brick oven, and in it Katherine baked pies and breads. When the bricks of the oven were very hot, the coals and ashes were swept out and then it was filled with the tasty treats to be baked.

"Hand me the peel," Katherine said, nodding at the long-handled shovel. "The pies there are ready to come out and there are more to go in."

As Katherine brought the hot pies out and put

in two more, Patsy filled a heavy iron pot called a Dutch oven with cornmeal dough and set it in the coals at the front of the fireplace. Cornbread was one of her favorite dishes, and Katherine was always willing to let her taste the crumbs when it was done.

Patsy and Katherine took a break at noon, sitting at the wooden table to snack on some raw vegetable scraps and bits of bacon that had cooked nearly black. The taste was sharp and wonderful. The Andersons, finished with their candle making, brought the tapers in for Patsy to replace in the bedrooms. They, too, sat down for a brief snack.

As Patsy and Katherine were testing the doneness of the cornbread, Mrs. Black peered into the kitchen. "The meal is nearly done? Fine." Then she said to Katherine, "Will my daughter make a good cook someday?"

Katherine patted Patsy on her mobcap and said, "I believe so! But her heart is truly in candle making, you know." She gave Patsy a wink.

Mrs. Black said, "Patsy, you may go now and play until I call for you."

Patsy said, "Thank you!" and hurried back to the stable to visit Barbara.

Patsy's Discovery

The dark-haired girl was in a stall grooming her pony, Little Bit. Sunlight sparkled through the stall's open window on the airborne dust. Little Bit nickered when she saw Patsy, who pulled out a piece of carrot she'd brought from the kitchen. The spotted puppy was sound asleep on a patch of sunlight near Little Bit's water bucket.

"Ah, you're going to teach my pony to bite," Barbara said lightheartedly as Patsy let Little Bit take the carrot from the palm of her hand. "She's already a feisty thing, hardheaded and stubborn."

"Not unlike a girl I know!" Mr. Layman called from down the stable aisle.

Barbara shook her head and laughed. She gave Little Bit a few more strokes with the curry comb, then put it into a pail with the other grooming tools. "She's done. Now I just have to take out the muck. Then we can find something fun to do."

Patsy helped Barbara carry the basket of old straw and manure to the compost pile beyond the paddock gate. Then they climbed onto the gate and stood side by side on the bottom slat of the gate, swinging back and forth. A squirrel dashed down the walkway and up a maple tree, then jumped across the stone wall to an oak in Mrs. Brubaker's yard.

"We could go visit your mother at Mrs. Boxler's shop," said Patsy after a moment. "There are always new hats to try on. And we could play with Abby Boxler if she isn't busy."

Barbara wrinkled her nose. "I'm too dirty to go calling at the milliner," she said. "I would have to change my dress and wash up. Let's think of something else."

"I could show you some more stitches," said Patsy. "I worked this morning on my sampler and it looks good. Would you like to practice with a needle? You'd be so much better with it if you'd only practice."

Barbara rolled her eyes. It was clear she didn't want to sew. Sometimes Patsy envied Barbara in that her mother didn't have time to make her sit still for writing and stitchery. At other times, though, Patsy wondered how Barbara would get on in life if she didn't learn housewifery.

Suddenly Barbara hopped off the gate. "I have an idea," she said. She went back to the compost pile and, using the pitchfork, scraped some muck back inside the basket. She carried the stinky load over to Patsy. "Let's play tea party!"

Patsy stepped down from the gate. "Tea party? We could do that. I have some old dishes in the tavern that Mother gave me so I can have parties with my doll."

"No!" said Barbara with a giggle. "I don't mean that kind of tea party. I mean let's pretend we are two girls in Boston, on the ships in the harbor."

Patsy scratched her nose. "I don't know what you're talking about."

"The brave Sons of Liberty rebelled against King George's unfair taxes, Patsy," said Barbara. "Don't you remember hearing of it? So many things had been taxed unfairly, including tea. Most people didn't want to pay the taxes on the tea but the British shipped the tea into Boston's port anyway. And so the Sons of Liberty went on board at night, dressed like Indians so no one would recognize them, and they threw the crates of tea into the water. The king was furious. The Sons of Liberty showed they wouldn't be forced into anything."

"Yes," said Patsy. "Henry and Father discussed it a little, but I don't recall much. I do remember that something like that happened here in Philadelphia before your family came. There was a ship named the *Polly,* loaded with tea, but the tea was not permitted to come ashore. It wasn't thrown into the water like the tea in Boston. But as I said, Father doesn't like us to talk about the troubles with the British in our home."

"But there is a war on," said Barbara. "How can he ignore that?"

"He chooses to," said Patsy. "Men in the tavern talk all the time, but Father won't stay to listen for more than a minute and won't have us engage in discussion with them. He won't even allow us to discuss the war when it is time for bed."

"Why? Your family isn't Quaker. I thought only Quakers refused even to discuss fighting."

Patsy shook her head. "I don't know why. But I don't think about the war much. There are too many other things to worry about."

"You would think of it if they began to fight here in Philadelphia," said Barbara. "My father says we must be ready. He says there are spies about all the time and we must be aware."

"Enough of this," said Patsy, waving her hand. "I don't want to talk about war now. So what is this game you want to play?"

"Okay," said Barbara. "We pretend that this basket is a crate of tea. We walk along the stone wall, holding it. Whoever gets as far as the harbor without dropping it wins."

Patsy wrinkled her nose. "I don't like that idea," she said. "First of all, that's manure in there."

"Yes! That way, we'll be very careful."

"Second of all, the wall belongs to Mrs. Brubaker, and you know how she feels about children."

"She won't see us," said Barbara. "She stays inside all the time."

Barbara carried the basket up the dirt path to the side garden. Patsy followed. She was glad that the view of the path was blocked from the backyard of the tavern by a row of spruce trees. Mother would certainly want to know what was going on with a muck bucket.

They went into the side garden, where their own bench would allow the girls to climb onto the top of the stone wall. Patsy first peeked in through the bedroom window to make sure neither of her brothers might be watching, then said, "You go first."

Barbara was very willing. She stepped onto the bench of the Black family garden and then pulled herself slowly onto the top of the wall.

The top is flat, luckily, but still, it isn't very wide, Patsy thought as she watched Barbara wobble a little before gaining her balance. *Maybe this isn't such a good game after all.*

"Here!" said Barbara. "Hand me the basket."

Patsy held the basket up. Barbara took it by the handles and began slowly walking the length of the wall. Her leather shoes clicked on the stone as she moved.

I hope Mrs. Brubaker is taking a nap, Patsy thought, following her friend.

Barbara reached the end of the side garden, then said, "I made it to the harbor! Now, Patsy, do you think you can make it this far?"

"I don't know," said Patsy, but the teasing in Barbara's voice convinced her she would certainly try, even if she was a bit nervous.

Barbara handed the basket to Patsy and jumped off the wall. The girls ran back to the bench, and Patsy climbed up.

The soles of her shoes were slippery; that was the first thing she noticed. The second thing she noticed was that she couldn't see her feet for the fullness of her skirt and petticoat. How was she to know if she was going to step off the wall if she couldn't see her feet? How had Barbara done it?

"Here," said Barbara. She passed the smelly muck basket to Patsy. "Now, let's see if you can hang on to that tea."

"I'm not certain I care for this game," Patsy said under her breath.

"Just look ahead, not down like that," said Barbara. "I watched the top of the stable in the distance. It helped me go straight."

Patsy took several steps, holding the basket tightly and watching the weather vane on the stable top. It did seem to help.

"Good!" Barbara exclaimed. "You would have been a fine Son of Liberty, carefully carrying his crate of tea across the deck of the ship and then dropping it right into the harbor. Splash! A wonderful mess!"

Patsy's jaw clenched. Her feet moved her slowly down the wall, feeling their way with pointed toes. She watched the weather vane. A bee buzzed past her ear and she shivered.

Suddenly a gust of wind blew up, throwing the weather vane into a spin and throwing Patsy off balance.

"Barb!" she shrieked.

"Be careful!" said Barbara.

But it was too late. The slippery soles of Patsy's shoes could not steady her, and the weight of the straw and manure in the basket shifted.

With a squeal, Patsy and the muck tumbled off the wall into Mrs. Brubaker's garden.

3

"Ooomph!" Patsy grunted as she hit the ground on her back. She covered her face quickly as the overturned muck basket dumped its contents on her head. "Oh, no!" she cried out.

A voice came from the other side of the wall. "Patsy, are you hurt?"

Patsy sat up, shaking her head. Manure and straw dropped from her head to her shoulders. The smell was atrocious. "Oh, Barb! I stink!"

"Are you hurt?"

"I don't think so. Let me stand up and see." Slowly Patsy reached out and took hold of a clump of boxwood and pulled herself to her feet. Her neck hurt, but not dreadfully. Her skirt was torn, and she could feel a lump swelling on her right knee. Other than that she was all right.

"I'm not hurt much," she said to Barbara. "I will have a time explaining my torn and filthy dress, however. I don't think I can mend it as quickly as I did my torn apron this morning."

"Is there a bench on that side? We have to get you out of there."

Patsy glanced around. She was actually inside Mrs. Brubaker's garden! It felt very strange indeed. And a little frightening. "No bench," Patsy said. "If you take my hands and I hop, maybe you can pull me over the wall."

"Give your hands to me, then," said Barbara. "And hop quickly before that woman comes out of her house."

Patsy reached over and grabbed Barbara. She put one foot against the wall and then pushed hard with the other to throw herself upward.

And then a hand grabbed her shoulder and pulled her downward.

"Patsy?" Barbara called from the other side of the wall. "What happened?"

But Patsy couldn't answer. She had been spun around and was staring into the face of the dreaded Mrs. Brubaker.

"What," the old woman hissed, her wrinkled face coming very close to Patsy's nose. "What are you doing trespassing in my garden, little girl?"

Patsy felt her mouth drop open, but she couldn't say a word. Her heart thundered madly in her chest like a horse running wild.

"Patsy, what is going on?" Barbara called.

Mrs. Brubaker's eyes were wide and furious. She shook Patsy sharply. "I said, what are you doing in my garden?"

Out of the corner of her eye, Patsy could see Barbara now. She had climbed up on the bench in the side garden and was staring agape at the old woman.

"I fell off the wall," Patsy stammered.

"And what were you doing on my wall in the first place?" the woman demanded.

Barbara's face fell away from the wall. *Maybe she's going to get help,* Patsy thought. *But who will she get? We'll both be in trouble for certain!*

"We were playing," Patsy managed.

"We will see about such play!" said Mrs. Brubaker. She practically lifted Patsy up from the ground, then walked her through the gate at the side of her house and out to the road. Patsy tried to keep up with the old woman's long strides.

Mrs. Brubaker didn't stop until they were on the tavern's marble stoop. She knocked and then stood back, never letting go of Patsy's arm.

The door opened. Katherine stood staring at the old woman and the manure-covered girl. "What is the matter?" she asked.

"I must see Mrs. Black this very minute," said Mrs. Brubaker.

"Certainly." Katherine disappeared, and a moment later, Patsy's mother was standing in the doorway, her eyes wide, her brows furrowed in a frown.

"Mrs. Brubaker," Mrs. Black said. "My goodness!"

"Goodness has nothing to do with it," Mrs. Brubaker said. "Your daughter has caused a great commotion in my garden and I want her to tell you all about it."

Mrs. Black looked at Patsy. Patsy looked at her mother. "I fell off the wall," she said. "We were only playing. I'm sorry."

"On my wall, spying into my garden," Mrs. Brubaker added. "And then leaping down to frighten me. What kind of manners are you teaching your children, Mrs. Black? Has a widow lady no right to be protected from such invasions?"

Mrs. Black sighed. "Patsy, have you nothing to say to our neighbor?"

Patsy muttered, "I'm sorry."

Then Mrs. Black nodded curtly at Patsy, directing her to come inside. Patsy stopped in the foyer and listened to the rest of the conversation, while Katherine slowly polished the banister on the stairs, her ear tipped in the direction of the door.

"I apologize for my daughter's behavior," said Mrs. Black. "I can't explain why she has shown such disrespect, but I will find the truth, I assure you. And we will handle her punishment appropriately."

"A whipping should do," said Mrs. Brubaker.

A whipping? thought Patsy. *For a silly accident? What a mean old woman you are, Mrs. Brubaker!*

"I assure you, we will take care of it, Mrs. Brubaker," Mrs. Black said in her most sincere tone. "Again, I'm sorry for this, and am sorry you had to bring my daughter home. Good day."

Mrs. Black shut the door and turned to Patsy. Katherine began rubbing the banister in earnest, looking everywhere but at the mother and daughter.

Patsy knew she wouldn't get whipped. Her parents didn't believe in raising their hands against

others, even children. But there would certainly
be punishment, and not something pleasant.

But before any more could be said, Mrs. Black
pinched her nose. "Gracious, and what have you
been rolling in?"

"Manure."

"Katherine, help Patsy get cleaned up right
away. I will not talk to someone who smells so
strongly of horses."

Katherine brought a clean set of clothing from
the Black family bedroom, then took Patsy out to
the kitchen and helped her wash in a large
wooden tub with warm water from the fireplace.
She put the dirty clothes aside to be scrubbed and
helped Patsy run a comb through her wet hair.

"Do I want to know what happened?" asked
Katherine.

"I'm not certain that you do. We were playing,
Barbara and I."

"And Mrs. Brubaker has a garden full of
muck?"

"No, we were playing *with* the muck."

"I declare!" said Katherine. But she was smiling. Then, with Patsy's hair done up again with
pins and covered with a clean mobcap, Katherine

said, "You'd best go have counsel with your mother."

Patsy went out across the yard to the tavern. Nicholas, who had been gone with Henry to the marketplace and the leather shop all day, was gathering wood from the stack in the yard for the fireplaces. He was blond, like his older sister, and slender. His short arms were stretched around several thick logs. He said, "Patsy! I heard you fell into manure!"

Patsy ignored him but her face flushed red. She went inside and met her mother in the Ulysses Room.

There were a few men seated at the tables, finishing their afternoon meal and lighting pipes. Patsy didn't want them to hear her chastisement. Luckily Mrs. Black didn't want them to hear it, either, because she led Patsy through the hall and the Red Horse Room and into the bedroom. She closed the door. Patsy sat on the straight-backed chair, staring at the toes of her scuffed shoes.

"Tell me what you were doing up on Mrs. Brubaker's wall," said Mrs. Black.

Patsy knew better than to lie. That would only make things worse. "Barbara and I were playing tea party."

"Tea party? On a wall?"

"Not a regular tea party. We wanted to see if we could carry a muck basket to the end of the wall without spilling it."

"But you called it a tea party?"

"Like in Boston a few years ago, Mother. We were the Sons of Liberty, and the muck basket was the tea crate."

Mrs. Black, clearly exasperated, waved her hand for Patsy to be silent. She took a deep breath and said, "For a full week beginning tomorrow, you shall have no afternoon playtime. Instead of going to the stable to visit Barbara and play with the puppy, you shall sit here for two hours in this very chair, and think about how you can better behave next time."

"A full week, Mother? I can't bear to sit still that long!"

"Would you have me take Mrs. Brubaker's suggestion of punishment?"

Patsy shook her head.

"You will also take a note of apology to our neighbor, and it will be a sincere note, Patsy. Also, I must inform Mr. Layman that Barbara was involved as well. He and his wife must see that Barbara understands the seriousness of disturbing a neighbor."

Sadly Patsy said, "Yes, ma'am."

"You are to compose yourself now, and then meet with the Anderson ladies in the Ulysses Room to clean up from the afternoon meal."

"Yes, ma'am."

Mrs. Black turned to leave. Then she stopped and said, "And, Patsy, your father would be distressed to hear that you were playing at war. In spite of the troubles we are facing with the British and the heated words we hear in our tavern from those who cheer the fighting, Mr. Black will not have his family share in such a sad, morbid interest. Do you understand?"

"Yes, ma'am," said Patsy, although she really didn't understand.

The door closed. Patsy felt tears spring to her eyes and she wiped them away. She hated to disappoint her mother. *But no time to cry now,* she thought to herself sternly. *It's all over. Now, to put my sampler away and go out to clean the Ulysses Room.*

Patsy looked at the windowsill where she had left her sampler to dry. It was gone. She looked on the floor. It wasn't there. *It's fallen into the side garden,* she thought. She leaned out the window to have a look.

The little spotted puppy was back again. His tail wagged madly at seeing Patsy in the window. But he wasn't digging holes this time. He had the sampler in his mouth, shredding and shaking it to pieces.

4

Sitting in the straight-backed chair for two hours at a time was one of the hardest things Patsy had ever done. She remembered learning to thread a needle and the many times she'd stuck her finger. She remembered learning to tighten the ropes evenly on the beds upstairs and learning to cook pudding without having it scorch. All those things had been difficult, but sitting still was by far the worst.

And it's worth nothing, she fumed. *What will I have learned other than it makes my back ache to sit so for such a long time? What good is that lesson, anyway? I should at least be able to start my new sampler, or work on my letters or read!*

Her mother had told her, "The lesson in this is never to be a bother to your neighbor, and that lesson will last you through your life."

If my back is ruined for sitting so long, Patsy thought sourly, *then it will surely be a lesson that will last my life. Won't they all be sorry when I can no longer stand straight and forever more must be carried around on a stretcher until I grow into a shriveled old woman and die?* She took a deep breath and let it out noisily.

Barbara had been given extra chores, and like Patsy, had to write a note to Mrs. Brubaker, apologizing. When Patsy delivered her note, no one answered the door. She had slipped the note under the door and gone home, relieved that she hadn't had to face the woman again.

Patsy dragged the soles of her shoes back and forth across the floor. She could hear men walking up and down the tavern stairs and back and forth in the upstairs bedrooms, and her own legs ached to be going somewhere. If she could do something it would make the punishment so much easier. Outside in the garden a mockingbird was perched in a holly bush, singing steadily in its many voices. Patsy tried to imitate the bird, but that was fun for only a few minutes.

If the puppy was inside he could keep her company. But the puppy had been confined to the stable on a rope now. With Patsy's ruined sampler and yet another hole in the side garden, this time by Mrs. Brubaker's wall, Patsy had sent a message to Barbara by way of Katherine, telling her that it didn't matter how much the puppy whined, he had to be tied up or Mr. Black would send him off for good.

A shiny black cricket hopped onto the windowsill and sat there chirping. Patsy watched it as it popped from the window and onto the family trunk against the wall. Although Patsy knew she was not allowed to get out of the chair, she leaned way over to try to catch it. It jumped behind the trunk.

"Bother," said Patsy. Then, staying in her chair, she scooted up to the trunk, pulled the doily off the top, and opened the lid. "I wonder what is in here," she thought aloud. She knew her mother kept some old family papers in the trunk, but there might be something of interest. Something to keep her mind off sitting still.

There were several papers, a deed for the tavern, some newspapers tied with string. And then

Patsy found a stack of letters addressed to her father. They had been written three years earlier.

I shouldn't read these, she thought. But she knew her mother had gone to the silversmith's and the apothecary with Nicholas, and Henry was out with Father. They would all be gone most of the afternoon. Katherine was in charge of the tavern for the next few hours. *If these letters weren't to be read,* Patsy reasoned, *then they would have been tossed out or burned in the fireplace.*

Slowly she opened the first letter. It had been sent from Philadelphia, from just across town.

She read softly.

Dear Andrew,

I pray this letter finds you and your family well. We have had the Illness close by for several days, but as of yet have warded it off with cleverness and stealth. The Illness is across the city as you well know. I have found a certain P. L., one I thought healthy, full of the sickness; watch for him as he may spread it to you if he comes to your tavern. Give him ale and tobacco but naught else.

Our friend in Virginia, R. F., writes that Illness is thriving there. Several shops which import items laced with the disease are now being avoided by wise shoppers. They believe this will help squeeze the Illness out. R. F. advises that we follow suit here to keep the problems at bay. I would say we should meet with our city friends and discuss this, but for me this would not be wise. As I have mentioned, the Illness lurks at my very door and I know it is a sometimes fatal malady. Therefore, watch carefully.

Illness will in no way keep me from doing what I must. It will in no way intimidate me from my good actions.

I shall write again soon.

> Your obedient servant,
> Thomas Hayes, S.O.L.

Patsy put the letter aside. It was a strange letter indeed. Nothing chatty, but nothing of urgency, either. Just a mention of a sick man who might come calling at the tavern. Yet what did "S.O.L." mean?" "Hmm," she said. She picked up a second letter. It, too, was from Philadelphia.

Dear Andrew,
I am hoping this letter finds you. It is sent

with the utmost care and caution by one free of the Illness and who will get it to you in haste. I will be moving to a northern city soon as the Illness is breathing down my neck and I fear being overcome. My family will not follow; please check in on them. Do not worry about me. I am fast enough to escape even a trouble such as this one.

I will contact you when I am safe and secure.

Your humble servant,
Thomas Hayes, S.O.L.

Patsy noticed the cricket. It had hopped to her foot, but she was no longer interested in catching it. She put the second letter aside. There was a third, with a different handwriting on the address. Patsy opened this one as well.

My dear Mr. Black,

I write with sorrow of the death of your friend, Mr. Thomas Hayes. He was overcome with an Illness before he reached Boston. I will explain more when I arrive in your city and visit you at your fine tavern.

Your obedient servant,
John Richard Sutton, S.O.L.

There was a thumping noise out in the Red Horse Room. With haste Patsy put the letters back into the trunk, replaced the doily, and scooted her chair over to the original spot on the floor. Just then her mother came in.

"I grow weary much too easily," said Mrs. Black, putting her hand to the small of her back and breathing heavily through her teeth. "I let Nicholas pick up the tonics I needed so I could come back and do simpler chores." Then she looked at her daughter and shook her head with a sad smile. "It aches me to see you so miserable. I wish the circumstances were different and there was no need for this."

"So do I," said Patsy.

"Just one more day," said Mrs. Black. "I will be so glad to have you free to play with Barbara."

"I will be, too," said Patsy. She watched while Mrs. Black went to the dresser and took out two long white baby gowns, gazed at them lovingly, then put them back. The tiny outfits were clothes that had been worn by all three of the Black children. Mrs. Black gave Patsy a quick kiss on the top of her head and left the room.

I need to know about those letters, Patsy thought. *I don't want to upset Mother but . . .*

Just then Henry came in carrying the cradle he'd been repairing. He gave Patsy a sad but humored shake of the head.

"Henry," said Patsy. "What do the letters S.O.L. stand for?"

Henry placed the cradle on the floor and looked at his little sister. "Father said we weren't to talk about this."

"About what?"

"About the war. S.O.L. stands for Son of Liberty. Where did you hear that abbreviation?"

"Oh, I just did. We live in a tavern; I hear all sorts of things." This wasn't exactly a lie, Patsy told herself.

Henry nodded, but Patsy could see his interest had picked up. His mouth twitched as if excited. Maybe Henry was a patriot, too.

"And what is the Illness?"

"The Illness is the oppression the Crown has put on us."

"I see," said Patsy.

"Don't let Father or Mother see," said Henry. "Let it be, Patsy."

Patsy nodded. Henry went out, closing the door quietly.

Patsy stared at the trunk. *Son of Liberty? Sons*

of Liberty were writing my father letters! What does this mean? Was my father involved in secret activities to work against the British, like the men who threw the tea into the Boston Harbor?

The cricket was by her foot. She scooped it up and looked into its tiny black eyes. "What do you think?" she asked it. "Is my father really a patriot, but doesn't want us to know?"

The cricket hopped away to the windowsill, then down into the side garden.

Patsy crossed her arms and looked back out the window at the trees, the flowers, and Mrs. Brubaker's wall. "I bet he is a patriot," she said. "But he believes he must keep it a secret, even from us."

She shivered with fear and excitement at the idea.

5

June had arrived and the new baby hadn't. Mrs. Black still bustled up and down the tavern steps, ordering her children and servants about, but Patsy could see she was moving slower than before, and her back seemed to be hurting her. The tavern was as crowded as usual, and the talk went relentlessly to the Congress meeting at the State House on Chestnut Street. Some men said the Congress should see the battles with the Crown as just flared tempers and that the Congress should do all it could to repair the damage with the mother country. Other men said the Congress should declare independence from England and have done with it. Patsy sometimes wished it was her place to pause and converse with some of the men, but it wasn't. She did her chores with mouth shut but curious ears open.

It was Friday evening, and there was to be a gala dance in the tavern's Ulysses Room. Although dances were held frequently, this was special. It was the annual summer-welcoming dance, and women who attended always wore brand-new summer outfits for the occasion.

Patsy loved seeing the women in their gowns. They would be of beautiful colors and fabrics such as silk, satin, and brocade. Sometimes they were trimmed in velvet. Although the war was on, women seemed able to find the proper materials, even if it meant tearing apart an old dress and making a new one from the cloth. The women wore satin slippers and always carried a fan. Katherine had explained to Patsy once that ladies spoke to gentlemen by moving their fans in certain ways. When Patsy wanted to know how, Katherine winked and said that when Patsy was older she would teach her.

Although Patsy was still too young to dance, she had permission to sit just outside the Ulysses Room in the hallway and watch. Her own feet would bounce in rhythm with the music as the men and women moved back and forth in the minuet, quadrille, and usually, as the night progressed and became more lively, a jig or two.

Preparations were ready for the evening. Chairs were lined up along the wall, and only one table remained in the Ulysses Room, to be stocked with food and drink. The other tables had gone into the Red Horse Room or the back. The floor had been scrubbed. Lanterns with fresh candles were on mantels and in windows. The quartet was settling in their corner, preparing to entertain with a violin, a flute, an oboe, and a small harpsichord.

"Mother," Patsy asked as she washed the last of the pewter mugs in a tub and put them aside on a linen towel for drying. They were in the small pantry in which the beers and spirits were kept for the customers. "May Barb come watch the dance with me tonight?"

Mrs. Black dried the mugs and set them upside down on the counter. There would be many attending the dance, and the Black family needed to know how large a crowd to expect. "Would she care to come? I thought young Miss Layman was more interested in outdoor games and such."

"Barb likes all kinds of things," said Patsy. "I've taught her some reading and some sewing, although truly those aren't her favorite pastimes. But she might well enjoy a dance. She's never attended. Could she please?"

Mrs. Black hesitated. Although her mother liked Barbara, Patsy could tell that the pause meant Mrs. Black wasn't sure Barbara would keep quiet and demure as she would be expected. And so Patsy said, "I will make certain she knows the rules, that she will sit like a lady and not laugh out loud."

"Very well," said Mrs. Black. "Please see she doesn't track stable mud into the hallway."

Patsy rinsed the last mug and then bounded out the back to the stable.

It was well past seven, and the sun was low in the sky, hanging like a bright eye over the trees and housetops of Philadelphia. Some horses were in the paddock, eating their rations of hay. The rest were bedded down in the stalls. The Laymans were not to be seen. Patsy guessed they were in their quarters over the stable. Holding the edge of her skirt, she climbed the wooden steps inside the stable to the second floor and tapped on the door off the small landing.

"Who is there?" came a call. It was Mrs. Layman.

"Patsy Black. May I please visit with Barbara for a moment?"

The door opened, and Patsy was welcomed into the Laymans' tiny parlor. Unlike the tavern, the furnishings in this home were very simple. The chairs were rough but covered in a nice, simple cloth; the rugs on the floor were woven and worn. The windows had simple hangings and no blinds. Slipware plates and platters rather than decorative ceramics sat on the mantel above the small fireplace. Set out on a table just big enough for four people were cold slices of ham, roasted potatoes, and beans waiting to be devoured.

Mrs. Layman said, "How nice to see you, Patsy. We are going to sit down to our meal. Would you do us the honor of joining us?"

Patsy said, "Thank you, ma'am, but no. I have had a meal just a short while ago, and we have been preparing for the dance ever since. I just came to ask Barb a question."

"Go on back, then," said Mrs. Layman.

Patsy walked to the door of the back room. In this, the only other room of the Laymans' home, the family slept on straw-stuffed mattresses. A lantern sat on a plain wooden table. Unlike the tavern, there were no paintings on the walls nor any looking glasses.

Grinning, Barbara jumped up from her chair. The puppy was in her arms, with a scrap of red ribbon around his neck. "I thought I heard you," Barbara said. "Did you come for supper?"

Patsy shook her head.

"Then did you come to play with the puppy? Do you like his bow? I've been keeping him inside at night, and then tied up during the day when I'm not watching him in the stable."

"No," said Patsy, giggling. "I came to ask you if you'd like to do something exciting!"

"Not like playing tea party, I hope."

Patsy laughed. "No, silly goose! I want to invite you to come watch the dance!"

Barbara's smile faltered a little, but Mrs. Layman came to the door, nodding enthusiastically. "What a kind offer, Patsy. Barbara should be delighted to come visit the tavern and observe the dancing."

Barbara set the puppy down and put her hands on her hips. "Mother, I don't think I should."

"And why not? You shall have a supper, then join Patsy. There are so few opportunities for you to see how fine ladies behave. This would be wonderful."

The puppy ran to Patsy. She picked him up and he snuggled into the crook of her arm. "It will be fun," she told her friend. "The music, the dancing! And Mother will let us share in the cakes if we are good. She will bring them right to us in the hallway."

"My dress is dirty," said Barbara. "My stockings have a long tear."

"And I know you have another dress," said Mrs. Layman. "I shall help you get ready." She turned to Patsy. "Thank you for the invitation. Barbara will be up at the tavern soon to join you."

Patsy giggled at Barbara's scowl. "Oh, don't pout," she said. "You know I'm going to try my best to make you into a lady."

"I feared as much," said Barbara. But then a smile found her face and she said, "We'll have some cake?"

Patsy nodded.

"I will see you there then, in a short while."

Patsy put the puppy down and left the household. She climbed down the steps and paused for a moment to pet Little Bit in her stall. "With a little coaching," she told the pony, "we shall soon have your mistress riding sidesaddle in proper form instead of bareback and astraddle."

The pony put her head against Patsy's hand, and Patsy gave her a quick pat. Then she headed back to the tavern, picking several red clovers from the side of the path leading to the backyard.

The Anderson sisters were still in the yard, folding linens that had been drying in the breeze. Usually they would have gone home by this time of night. Only Katherine stayed to help the Blacks manage the dances. But the women were moving slowly this evening, folding and refolding towels before putting them into the linen basket. Neither one spoke to the other, which was not the norm, either. Although the women were somber, they most often talked to each other in their soft monotonic voices.

"Good evening," Patsy said.

The sisters looked up from the folding. Martha said, "Good evening, miss." Molly nodded and then looked back at the cloth in her hands.

Patsy suddenly felt sorry that the women had so much to do that they would be late returning home. She tucked the clover flowers into the pocket of her apron and said, "I see you have quite a bit of folding to do. I could help you for a few minutes if you'd like, to hasten it along."

But Molly shook her head adamantly. Patsy was surprised to see an expression of something other than tedium on her face. Molly said, "No, miss, that will not be necessary. Thou art kind to offer, however."

Martha echoed her sister's sentiment. "Thou need not take time away from what thy mother would have thee do. But we do thank thee."

Patsy nodded. "Very well, then. Good evening."

"Good evening, miss," the sisters said together.

Patsy entered the tavern and went down the hall. She peeked into the Ulysses Room. The musicians adjusted their chairs and chatted quietly. The violinist drew his bow across his strings, tilting his head to listen to the tone.

"This will be a grand evening," Patsy said to herself. She walked through the Red Horse Room, in which a few men were smoking and talking, and into the family bedroom. Mrs. Black was there sitting on the chair, looking out at the side garden.

"Mother?" Patsy asked as she closed the door. "Are you ill?"

"No, dear," said Mrs. Black. "Only weary. But Henry arrived from his long day at the market just a short time ago. He and Nicholas are with your father, ready to manage the dance. He gave me leave to rest."

"You won't attend the dance?" asked Patsy. "You always tell me about the ladies, who they are and where they come from. You tell me who is dancing correctly and who has the stumble-foot. It's all so much more cheerful if you are there."

Mrs. Black smiled and held out her arms. Patsy went into them for a long, warm embrace. "Thank you, Daughter," Mrs. Black said. "But the baby is insisting I retire early tonight. And I can't argue with your little sister."

Patsy grinned. "Sister?"

"Oh, I'm just supposing," said Mrs. Black. "I will be so happy with a boy or a girl. But I do know your preference."

Patsy nodded and stood up. She took the wilting red clovers from her pocket and gave them to her mother, who thanked her. "I must change into clean clothes now," Patsy said. "Barb is going to join me to watch."

In just a matter of minutes, Patsy was in her nicest dress, pale blue with embroidered flowers her mother had sewn on the bodice. There was lace at the neck and on the sleeves. Her mopcap was gone, and in its place a lacy blue bonnet.

"What a lady you are, Patsy!" said Mrs. Black. "Now, remind yourself that you are. And remind Barb, too, lest she forget."

"I will, Mother," said Patsy. She skipped to the Red Horse Room, got two chairs, and put them in the hall, out of the way of the men and women who were just beginning to arrive for the festivities.

Music began. Women sat daintily in chairs, fanning. Once again, Patsy wished Katherine or her mother thought her old enough to know the silent language of the fan. Few women wore the hip-enlarging farthingales now, as many saw them as symbols of Toryism and loyalty to the Crown. Their skirts were full but took up much less space than they once had. The men walked nearly as daintily as the women, moving about, talking with each other, bowing politely and dabbing at their noses with handkerchiefs. Their wigs were of various shades, from darkest black to powdered white.

I wonder if there are any Sons of Liberty here tonight, Patsy thought suddenly. It was a strange idea, and she found herself studying the men more intently. Of course, the Sons of Liberty no longer existed. They only performed their defiant acts years back.

But is that right? Are there men even today who, even if they don't actually fight, do things secretly to help out the patriots?

"Hello!"

Patsy turned to see Barbara. She had come up the hall very quietly and now stood, hands behind her back.

"My goodness, Barbara! I would not have recognized you for that outfit," said Patsy.

Indeed, Barbara looked like a lady. Her dress was pink, with gathers and tatting. Her face was freshly scrubbed, making the freckles stand out against her pink cheeks. Her black hair had not one strand out of place beneath her white bonnet. A sprig of fresh purple lilac was pinned to the side of the bonnet.

Barbara sat down on the chair next to Patsy. She folded her hands in her lap, but her feet crossed and uncrossed.

"Sit still," said Patsy.

"I can't," said Barbara. "I am not used to wearing stays, but Mother said a lady must get used to them. She said I've grown up missing much of what I should know, and that tonight is a good time to begin learning."

Patsy wrinkled her nose and smiled. Barbara was right about stays. Her own could chafe something mightily at times. But she was used to them.

"What do we do?" Barbara asked.

"We watch the dancers," said Patsy. "See there, they are beginning a minuet. Isn't it lovely? They have such grace, don't you think? Mother has taught me some of the steps, but I'm not old enough to join the evening dances."

"How old must you be? If you can dance, you should be able to join them, I would think."

"Father says sixteen."

"Hmm," said Barbara.

They sat, talking quietly and watching the dancers. Soon Patsy's older brother, Henry, with dark hair like his father's and green eyes like his mother's, brought out cakes on a small plate and cups of punch. "You ladies appear to be in need of refreshment," he said.

"And you, sir, appear to be dandy enough to join the dancers," said Patsy.

"Thank you, madam," said Henry. With a little bow, he returned to his duties in the pantry.

After viewing several minuets and a hearty jig, Barbara said, "I must visit the necessary."

"All right, but be quick about it," said Patsy.

Barbara was gone only a minute, when she was back with a funny grin on her face.

"What is it?" asked Patsy.

"Come with me and see," said Barbara. "But you must come without a sound."

Patsy stood and quietly followed Barbara down the hall and out the back door. On the step outside, Barbara stopped and held her finger to her lip. Then she stepped to the ground and peered out from behind a bush. She motioned for Patsy to do the same.

No wonder they were taking their time with the linens! Patsy thought. *They wanted to watch the dance.*

The baskets were full, the linens folded neatly, but the Anderson sisters were still there. But they weren't working; they were standing by the tavern wall, hands pressed to the brick, peering in the window of the Ulysses Room. Lantern light pooled around their faces and shoulders, and their mouths were set in their usual serious line. But at the bottom of the plain gray skirts the women wore, Patsy could see dancing feet. They moved side to side, back and forth, with tiny little skipping steps, all so subtle that one would have to look at their shoes to notice any movement at all.

So, the solemn, humorless ladies have a cheerful side after all, Patsy thought.

Barbara nudged Patsy and put her hand to her mouth to keep from laughing out loud. Patsy smiled, then went back inside the tavern while Barbara made her way to the necessary behind the kitchen.

As she sat on her chair in the hall and looked at the dancing men and women, Patsy thought about how it was hard to know what was going on in another's mind sometimes. If a person stays quiet and doesn't tell, how would you know?

How would I know which of the gentlemen in the tavern at this moment favor the British?

How would I know the Anderson ladies really love dancing, although their religion forbids it?

And how would I know my father had been a Son of Liberty, as he is determined to keep it a secret?

"I suppose you just can't know a person until you know him," Patsy said to herself. And then she took a bite out of a piece of butter cake, and it was luscious.

6

"Patsy!"

The voice came from out the window in the side garden. It was midmorning, and Patsy was trying her hardest to get a new sampler right. She had told her mother about the other one falling from the window and being destroyed, but hadn't admitted that the puppy had chewed it up. She was going to make sure the new one was perfect.

Patsy got up from the chair and looked out. Barbara stood a few paces away, wringing her hands.

"Gracious, Barbara, you look like you've seen a banshee!"

"Worse," said Barbara. "It's your puppy."

"Where is he?"

Barbara pointed tentatively at Mrs. Brubaker's stone wall. "In her garden," she said.

"No! How did that happen?"

"I have no idea. But I heard the barking when I was walking Little Bit. I followed the sound and came into your garden. I stood up on the bench and . . ." She stopped and shook her head. "He's in there, digging in Mrs. Brubaker's flowers."

Patsy climbed out of the window. After brushing herself off, she ran to the bench and peeked over the wall. The puppy wasn't visible, but she could hear his occasional yip.

"What are we going to do, Barb?"

"I don't know!"

"We have to get him out."

"How? He won't come when I call."

Patsy took a deep breath. This was the last thing she needed to deal with. In a whisper, she called, "Come here, puppy!"

There was no sound except for the bluejays in Mrs. Brubaker's trees. And then Patsy heard the sound of scratching in dirt not far away.

"Come here, you stubborn mule!" Patsy's voice was a little louder. She glanced at Mrs. Brubaker's back door. Maybe the woman was taking a nap.

If Patsy climbed over and grabbed the puppy, and Barbara pulled her out right away, no one would know. Patsy wouldn't get in trouble and the puppy wouldn't be sent away.

"Barb, I'm going over to get him," Patsy said.

"Are you sure? If you get another dress dirty and your stockings torn, your mother will stop letting us play together. You don't want to sit in that chair for another week, do you?"

"No."

"Let me go, then. I'm always getting dirty. I'll climb over and you help me back."

Patsy thought only for a moment. She knew Barbara had a good point. Barbara was always covered in smudges. She said, "All right. But hurry. We can't let Mrs. Brubaker find out we're back in her garden yet again."

Barbara climbed onto the bench, then rolled over the wall. She dropped down, crouched, and looked back up at Patsy. "Where is your brother Nicholas?"

"The Anderson sisters are tutoring him in the kitchen. They won't let him free of his lessons for at least another half hour or so. Father's gone to the printer with Henry. Mother is visiting with Mrs. Boxler in the Red Horse Room."

"Good," said Barbara. "We have a few minutes, then." She crawled out of sight behind a
long clump of hedges.

Patsy crossed her arms on the wall and put her
chin down. Her gaze traveled back and forth between Mrs. Brubaker's back door and where Barbara had disappeared. She began to count. *One,
two, three, four, five.*

"Hurry, Barb, just pick up the puppy and come
out!" she whispered.

Six, seven, eight, nine, ten.

Mrs. Black could be heard at the back of the
tavern, calling for Katherine. *I hope she doesn't
come to the bedroom looking for me,* Patsy
worried.

Eleven, twelve, thirteen.

"Barb! Hurry up!" Patsy hissed. "Oh, please
hurry."

Suddenly from somewhere within the garden,
behind the brush and shrubs where Patsy couldn't
see, she heard a rustling and a thumping sound
and then stillness. Patsy swallowed hard.

Barb? What happened?

Patsy looked at the window to the bedroom.
She looked back into Mrs. Brubaker's garden. *I*

can't wait any longer, she thought. *I have to go get the puppy and see if Barb is all right.*

Trying to keep her stockings from snagging on the stone, Patsy pulled herself up and over the wall.

Back on her feet inside Mrs. Brubaker's garden, Patsy felt dizzy. She remembered falling with the muck basket, and how frightened she was when Mrs. Brubaker had found her. The garden looked pretty from the outside, but it felt cold and ominous from the inside.

Patsy bent over and tiptoed along the thick hedges. She peered out through thinned branches, looking for her friend and the puppy. *Where are they? This doesn't make any sense at all!* She went around the end of the hedges and paused to look up and down a brick walkway, down to the trellis, and up toward the steps to Mrs. Brubaker's back door.

"Barb?" Patsy called hesitantly. She didn't see her friend or the dog. Had Barbara fainted somewhere behind a rosebush or a clump of tall azaleas? Patsy crept out onto the brick walkway and moved toward the thickest patch of roses.

"Barb? Barb? Barb?"

Then she heard whining, and looked up at Mrs.

Brubaker's back door. The puppy was there, tied to a rope. The rope was tied to the branch of a small tree.

How did he get tied up? Patsy wondered. Her heart began to pick up speed. *What had happened?*

"Barb!" she called. "Barb, Barb!"

Then Mrs. Brubaker popped up from behind the roses, her face twisted in a furious scowl, one angry finger pointing and shaking at Patsy. "You, child!" she shrieked. "You come into my garden uninvited once more."

Patsy's mouth dropped open. She stood paralyzed, unable to speak. *Oh, dear, not again!* Patsy thought.

"This is inexcusable! We'll just see what your parents have to say about this second infraction. We'll just see who will be able to sit down for the next month."

"Mrs. Brubaker," Patsy began. "Please let me explain what . . ."

But Mrs. Brubaker jerked Patsy's arm sharply. "I will not listen to your silly chatter. Impudence! I'll take you home once more, and will demand that you and your family leave me alone. I have a right to be left alone."

Mrs. Brubaker took Patsy home. As they left the garden, Patsy spied Barbara behind a box-wood, crouched down and hiding with one hand to her mouth so she wouldn't make a sound.

It's always me getting caught! Patsy thought, dismayed. She didn't try to squirm from the woman's grip; it would have done no good. She knew she was in serious trouble and that it would be useless to fight it.

The tavern door was opened by Katherine, who glanced at Mrs. Brubaker, then at Patsy, and said, "Again, Patsy?"

Patsy looked at the marble step and felt tears well in her eyes.

"Mrs. Black, please," said Mrs. Brubaker.

"Will you please come in, Mrs. Brubaker?" asked Katherine. "You are very welcome, and the sun is quite bright out there."

But Mrs. Brubaker said, "No, thank you. Please get Mrs. Black."

Katherine withdrew. Patsy continued to stare at the step. She heard talking, then her mother's exasperated groan. Then she heard the door swing open wider, and her mother say, "Mrs. Brubaker, I am mortified to find you here again with my Patsy. Pray, tell me what has happened this time and how we can right this offense."

Mrs. Brubaker jerked Patsy's arm, and Patsy looked up. Tears flowed down her cheeks to the kerchief around her neck. "This girl came into my garden once more," the old woman said. "Without invitation, without cause."

"Patsy!" said Mrs. Black.

"But to make matters worse," said Mrs. Brubaker, "your daughter was barking at me!"

"Excuse me?" said Mrs. Black.

"What?" said Patsy.

"Barking at me! Such cruel taunting! 'Bark, bark, bark!' she said. Several times. I cannot tell you how upset I am, Mrs. Black."

"Barking?" asked Mrs. Black. She cupped Patsy's chin and searched her daughter's face for an answer.

"Mother, I did no such thing!" said Patsy.

"Hush, child. You have not been asked to speak," said Mrs. Brubaker.

"Patsy," said Mrs. Black, her voice tight and stern. "Why were you in Mrs. Brubaker's garden?"

Patsy bit her lip. She could only tell the truth, as hard as it would be to do. She said, "I went to get the puppy. He'd somehow gotten in there. I fear he's dug a hole."

"An excuse to come in and bark at me!" said Mrs. Brubaker. "Mrs. Black, you must do something with this willful child. I cannot endure more of these disturbances and insults. And I tell you, that child will not see that puppy ever again."

"What are you to do with the puppy?" asked Patsy.

"I shall keep the animal!"

"Oh, I am very sorry about being in your garden, Mrs. Brubaker," said Patsy. "But don't keep the puppy!"

Mrs. Brubaker turned and stormed off toward her house.

But I didn't bark! Patsy thought. *Why are you thinking I did? And it isn't fair to keep the puppy!*

Patsy was sent to the bedroom and had to wait until dinnertime before her father and mother could both talk with her. It was a very long wait indeed. When her parents came in, she sat straight and looked them in the eye. She knew what she would say, and they would hear her out.

Both Mr. and Mrs. Black stood, arms crossed. Father removed his hat and tilted his head back. Such a handsome man, but such a stern look. *But no matter,* Patsy thought. *He must listen to me! He must!*

"You were in Mrs. Brubaker's garden again," said Mr. Black.

"Yes, Father, I was."

"Tell me why."

"I must admit it was the puppy again. He found a patch of loose soil by her wall and dug beneath it. I went to get him so he would not ruin her flowers and shrubs."

"Mmm," said Mr. Black. "And now your mother tells me you barked at the woman."

"No! I did not! Her ears are not what they should be, for there was no barking except for the puppy. I only called for Barbara while I was in her garden. I only said, 'Barb, Barb, Barb, Barb.'"

Patsy looked at Mr. Black. Mr. Black looked at Mrs. Black. Mrs. Black looked at Patsy and burst out laughing. Patsy couldn't believe her ears. Her mother was laughing!

"I'm sorry," said Mrs. Black, putting a hand to her mouth and trying to stop the giggles.

Patsy felt a giggle bubble up in her own chest. "I can see now how she thought it," she said. "But I didn't bark!"

Even Mr. Black was smiling now, although he was trying not to. He said, "This doesn't excuse the matter of trespassing, Patsy."

"No," Patsy said. "I'll write an apology. I'll do extra chores. I'll sit in this chair for two weeks."

"You may well do that," said Mr. Black.

"But Mrs. Brubaker isn't excused for keeping my puppy, either."

Both Mr. and Mrs. Black frowned. "I dare say, Patsy," said Mr. Black, "that you have nothing to say on the matter."

Patsy felt her throat go dry. But she had to speak up. She glanced at the trunk and thought of the letters she'd read. "Father, I do have something to say. Please listen to me. It isn't fair to keep something which doesn't belong to you. The puppy shouldn't have gone in Mrs. Brubaker's yard. I know that. But to keep the puppy and expect us to say nothing because we're afraid is bad. The British have taken our money in taxes for years without our consent. You know this."

"Patsy . . ." began her mother.

"That old lady will in no way intimidate me for my good actions," said Patsy.

Mr. Black's mouth dropped open. He ran his

fingers along the brim of the hat in his hands. "What did you say?"

"She will in no way intimidate me for my good actions. I read those words, Father. And I think they are true. Don't you?"

"Where did you read those words?"

"In a letter."

Mr. Black suddenly slammed his hat down on the bed and knelt on the floor in front of Patsy. His face flushed red. Taking Patsy firmly by the shoulders, he said, "In what letter did you read those words?"

"A letter in the trunk," Patsy said quietly.

Mr. Black looked at the floor.

"You were a Son of Liberty, weren't you, Father? Is that not what S.O.L. stands for?"

Slowly, Mr. Black nodded. "But Daughter, it is something of the past. I do not want to talk about that time."

Patsy pressed on, feeling more brave, but keeping her words steady and slow. She didn't want to say anything to cause her father pain. "Surely you understand what I'm saying. I hear the men in the tavern, talking about our struggles. I cannot help but do so. And even though this is just a dog, I see that it is much the same in the unfairness of it. I was wrong to go into her yard. But she is wrong to keep something which does not belong to her."

Mrs. Black came over to Patsy and put one hand on her husband's shoulder, one on her daughter. "Patsy, he doesn't want to speak of it anymore."

Mr. Black stood up. He said, "I will tell you, Patsy. I have no need to hide it since your discovery. I was a Son of Liberty two years back. I was instrumental in getting information back and forth along the city and into the hands of those who would fight on the front line. But my friend Thomas Hayes was caught just outside of Boston by the British troops and hanged for being a spy. He had on him a message of 'disloyalty to the Crown.' I was deeply grieved to hear of his death. He was a fine friend. I decided it had come too close to me. I had no idea what it was I was handling. The whole business of fighting England was like struggling with a snake, Patsy. A poisonous, murderous snake. And so I vowed to remain neutral, like the Quakers. Let the war go on around us, and what happens, happens. I will not be part of it."

Patsy stood up and gave her father a hug. "I'm sorry that I made you sad," she said.

"But I see that you are concerned with fairness, Patsy. When your time of punishment is over, you have my permission to ask Mrs. Brubaker for the puppy back. I don't know if she will give it back, but you may ask."

Patsy smiled and bounced on her toes. "Thank you!"

But Mr. Black retained his serious expression. "I said after the punishment. And again, Mrs. Brubaker may well decide not to give it back. Why would she want to? Try to see it from her point of view."

And with that, Mr. Black left the bedroom. Mrs. Black went to the fireplace, took a taper, and touched the wick to the glowing coals. She then lit the candles on the mantel.

"This time," she said, turning to her daughter, "you will not go in the trunk while you are sitting still. You will sit ten days this time. In addition, you will write Mrs. Brubaker a note, and every day you will bake something in the kitchen with Katherine and take it to our neighbor in a gesture of repentance."

"Yes, Mother," said Patsy.

"And shall this be it? Shall this be enough to remind you to stay where you belong?"

"Yes, Mother."

"Now, chores. After that, your note."

"Yes, Mother."

Mrs. Black linked arms with her daughter and the two walked into the Red Horse Room, where Patsy was put immediately to scrubbing the floor. But Patsy had a lot on her mind, and the work seemed to fly by. She had a new game for herself and Barbara just as soon as her free time was returned to her.

She had a new game that would be more fun and exciting than anything Barbara had come up with. She only hoped Barbara was brave enough to try!

7

"I've thought of a new game," said Patsy. She and Barbara were in the side yard, sitting next to each other on the bench, having a real tea party with the set of chipped, cast-off dishes her mother had given her for play. There was water in the cups dipped from a small puddle from last night's shower. Even though Barbara wasn't fond of quiet games, sometimes she seemed to enjoy being in the garden, just talking and pouring cups of water for the dolls. The dolls, Mrs. Byrd and Sallie Jones, were propped up against a boxwood hedge, their painted faces watching the proper motions of their hostess. Both the dolls belonged to Patsy.

The afternoon sun was very hot. It was mid-June, and dust was heavy in the city, floating from the street to the side garden and coating everything with a fine layer. It was hard to keep the tavern clean in the summer; sometimes the clothes and linens on the line in the backyard would have to be scrubbed all over again.

"A new game?" asked Barbara. "I don't suppose it involves walking on Mrs. Brubaker's stone wall."

"No," said Patsy, shaking her head quite forcefully. Her hat wobbled a little, the ribbon beneath her chin tugging. She would have liked to take it off, as there was plenty of shade in the garden, but Mother would not hear of it. Her daughter should never let sun spoil her lovely complexion. Then Patsy lowered her voice and leaned forward. Barbara leaned forward, too, her eyes growing bright with excitement. "But it does involve Mrs. Brubaker," Patsy whispered.

Barbara sat back again. "I can't believe my ears, Patsy Black!"

"Listen," said Patsy. "Hear me out. I miss my puppy, and I know you do, too. Mrs. Brubaker has had the dog for a week and a half now, and

I don't think it's fair for her to keep what doesn't belong to her."

"Yes," said Barbara. "But it was in her garden. I suppose she has the right to keep it."

"Now I am sounding like you and you are sounding like me," said Patsy. "It is always you who wants to be daring, to speak your mind and make demands. Now think. If a stray horse wandered into our paddock, would we feel free to keep it just because it stood on our land?"

Barbara thought for a moment, then shook her head. "But a dog isn't a horse."

"No. But fairness is fairness. Should the British be allowed to take taxes from us just because they think they own the land on which we live?"

"Patsy! Don't let your father hear you talking like that."

"Don't worry. Now answer me. Do you think those taxes are fair?"

"No, I don't believe they are. My mother and father don't, either."

"All right! I want to form a club. We can call ourselves the Daughters of Liberty. We can do good deeds for people in secret. And the first thing we can do is a good deed for my puppy, and that is to rescue him from unfair imprisonment at Mrs. Brubaker's."

Barbara stood up from the bench and said, "What mysterious gnat has bitten you, Patsy, and made you lose your head? Go to Mrs. Brubaker's? I don't want to think about it."

"I do. I've been to her house every day this past week, taking her buns and breads. She's answered my knock and taken the food but has said not a word. In all truth, I've been afraid to say something on my own, but if you were with me I'd be all the braver."

"I'm not certain, Patsy."

"Please?"

Barbara climbed on the bench and stood looking into the neighbor's garden. Then she spun around, almost toppling. "It's scary, but I do fancy the idea after all. Daughters of Liberty! I like the sound of it."

"Let me put away my dolls and dishes," Patsy said. "Then we will go to her house. I will not be unkind, but I will make my statement clear."

"And brave!" said Barbara.

"And brave," said Patsy, and she knew she would be.

But as the two girls stood on the step before

Mrs. Brubaker's door, each waiting for the other to summon the courage to knock, Patsy wasn't feeling so brave anymore. How hard this was, speaking one's mind and taking the chance of being scolded or worse. And how much harder it must have been for the Sons of Liberty, taking their lives in their hands for the purpose of justice and freedom.

This is justice and freedom for my puppy, Patsy reminded herself. She took a deep breath and knocked on the door.

"I hope she isn't home," said Barbara in a sudden, quiet voice.

"She's home," said Patsy. "I saw her go into the house not a quarter hour ago."

They waited, heads tilted, trying to hear footsteps inside the big house. All they could hear were baby birds chirping in Mrs. Brubaker's bird bottle on the side of her house and the horses and carriages on the street behind them.

Patsy knocked again. She listened. There was no sound inside.

"She's not home," said Barbara.

"Yes, she is. She just won't answer our knock," said Patsy. She knocked a third time, then said, "I suppose we'll have to try again later." She was relieved yet disappointed. How could the Daughters of Liberty demand something in the name of fairness when Mrs. Brubaker wouldn't even come to her door?

The girls walked back to the tavern and stopped on the step. "What will we do now?" asked Barbara. "This isn't much of a game, Patsy."

"Come with me."

The girls went into the tavern, through the Red Horse Room, and to the family's bedroom. Patsy found paper, pen, and ink. There wasn't room for two girls to sit at the small table so they sat on the floor, even though Patsy knew her mother wouldn't approve of young ladies doing such. Patsy carefully tucked her skirt so it would wrinkle as little as possible.

"We need a code," Patsy said. "We need to be able to write to each other in a way that no one else can decipher what it is we're saying. This way we can send messages."

Barbara nodded and rubbed her hands together. "Yes!" The girls sat in silence for a moment, looking at each other. Then Barbara said, "But how will we do it?"

"I don't know," said Patsy. "But how about

this." She leaned over the paper and carefully dipped the pen into the ink and began to draw. She made an apple, then a bird bottle, then a cow, then a door. "We can draw things for different letters, *A, B, C, D,*" she said, sitting straight so Barbara could see. "Then we make words from the pictures."

Barbara said, "That's too complicated. It would take forever to make a sentence."

"Hmm," said Patsy. "You're right. Do you have an idea?"

"Have you a small looking glass?"

Patsy hopped up and looked in the dresser. Her mother had one, set in brass. She sat back down and handed it to Barbara.

"Look," said Barbara. "If we hold the glass to the paper and write as we peer in it, we can make the words backward. Then someone would need another looking glass to hold up to the message to read it."

"But we might be in a place where we have no looking glass."

Barbara nodded. "So what shall we use for a code?"

They both thought for a moment. Then Patsy said, "Let's have *A* mean *Z,* let *B* mean *Y,* let *C* mean *X*. Each letter can represent the opposite letter in the alphabet."

Both girls agreed this would be fine. They wrote the code down twice and tore the paper in half, and each tucked the piece into her skirt pocket.

Patsy returned to her chores for today, which consisted of spinning flax in the corner of the kitchen, dusting, and walking with Nicholas to the home of Mr. and Mrs. Samuel Johnson on Sassafras Street to take a berry pie. Mr. Johnson had broken his leg and was recuperating, and so it was common kindness to remember them with a visit and a gift. They sat with Mr. and Mrs. Johnson for a few minutes and chatted, then returned home. Nicholas, of course, wanted to stop in every shop along the way. Patsy said, "Nicholas, we don't have money with which to make a purchase. Why do you vex me so with your constant requests to stop?"

"Because it's fun!" he replied, and she could only smile. She enjoyed visiting Boxler's Milliner and the wig maker's shop, even though she had no money for a new hat and even though her father was the only one to occasionally wear a wig.

*　　*　　*

Patsy's Discovery

It was nearing dinnertime when Patsy and Nicholas arrived at Black's Tavern. Men were all over, taking their belongings upstairs to claim a sleeping space, playing cards in the Red Horse Room, and sitting at tables in both the downstairs rooms, talking loudly with laughter and occasional grunts of anger. Nicholas was set to the task of drawing water and bringing it in with the firewood. Henry was in the backyard splitting the logs. Patsy and Katherine brought in steaming platters of pork, breads, bacon, headcheese, chicken, jellies, and beans. They served the men, staying close enough that they could hear what the men needed, but far enough that the men didn't feel the females were eavesdropping on their conversations. However, it was hard not to hear a lot of it.

"They are still arguing this very minute," said one man, jabbing the air with the tip of his pipe. "They can't decide how to do what they should do. And that is declare independence and have it done with. We are already at war. We should go ahead and admit it to ourselves!"

"Many in the Continental Congress don't want to call it war," said another man, slamming his bread down to his pewter plate. The plate rattled for a moment on the tabletop. "They want to talk,

to compromise with the Crown. It's not too late
to smooth this over and bring a peace with which
we can all live."

"It is too late."

"It's not. Not while a single man lives."

"A single man shan't live, or should not want to
live, under the oppression we have experienced!"

One man snatched up his plate and moved to
another table.

And so the evening went, the conversations
going from topic to topic, and usually returning
to the war. Tempers ebbed and flowed.

The night was busier than usual. Not only were
there more men, but the absence of Patsy's
mother was evident. She was in the bedroom rest-
ing. When dinner was over, the dishes cleared,
and the men either smoking in candlelight or re-
tired upstairs, the Black family retreated to their
bedroom. Mr. Black recited evening prayers and
read from the Bible, and then the family got into
bed. As Patsy pulled out her trundle bed, she saw
in the dim light of the hearth's glow a small piece
of paper. What was it?

When her family was asleep, she crept to the
fireplace and held the paper down to see. It was
a message from Barbara. How did it get inside on

her bed? Patsy looked at the window and smiled. Barbara was a far more clever and quick climber than Patsy would ever be.

The note read, "Meet me in the stable tomorrow at noon."

Patsy climbed back into bed, tucked her arms beneath her head, and wondered what adventure Barbara had in mind for the next day.

8

Barbara had an armful of hay which she was bringing out to two horses in the paddock when Patsy arrived, flushed and smiling.

"Hello!" Patsy said. She hopped onto the gate and let her arms dangle over it. "I found that message last night. You are a good Daughter of Liberty with your stealth and silence. What the British wouldn't give for a spy such as yourself to take messages back and forth."

"I nearly was caught," Barbara said as she lay the hay down and one horse, a large chestnut mare, brought her nose over to sniff and then take some in her mouth. "Henry came into the room and I ducked behind the bed. He was only there for a book, however, and didn't look around and see me. My heart pounded so, I thought it would pop right out!"

Patsy laughed. "Ah, and had you been caught for trespassing, you would have to sit in a chair for hours, too."

Barbara grinned. She stroked the horse's nose and came to the gate.

"So tell me," said Patsy. "Why did you want to meet me? Is it something exciting?"

"I know how to get the puppy back." Barbara's hazel eyes danced with eagerness.

"We tried yesterday. We could do the same today, but Mrs. Brubaker might well know it is us again and not answer. She's such a bitter woman!"

"She doesn't have to know it is us!"

"What are you saying?"

"We dress in boys' clothes and go to the door. Mrs. Brubaker peeks out and believes it is someone else. She opens the door and we say we are two boys who live near the river. We say we've lost our spotted puppy only weeks ago, and has she seen him?"

"Gracious!" Patsy exclaimed. "We can't do such a thing."

Barbara's brows came together. "Why not?"

"Because it's not fair."

"Does that matter? Holding on to the puppy isn't fair of Mrs. Brubaker."

"No, but I don't think we should try to stop unfairness with unfairness. It's like lying or cheating."

Barbara rubbed her nose. She dragged the tip of her shoe along the dust, then said, "Maybe you are right. I thought it was a fine idea, though."

Patsy patted her friend on the arm. "And we should still ask for the puppy. Will you go with me once more?"

"I suppose."

The girls went back to Mrs. Brubaker's house. Once again, Patsy knocked and there was no answer. "Perhaps this time she has truly gone out," whispered Barbara.

"Perhaps." Patsy knocked again. While she waited listening, Barbara leaned over and peered in the window by the door. And then she spun back around, her eyes wide.

"Patsy! Something is wrong with Mrs. Brubaker! She is lying on her foyer floor!"

Patsy ran to the window. She held her hand up

to the glass and squinted. Indeed, there on the floor, not moving, lay the old woman.

"Try to open the door!" said Barbara.

Patsy tugged, but the door was locked. "What should we do?"

"She must have a doctor. We must tell your mother and then run for Dr. Willard right away."

They raced to the tavern and burst in through the door. "Mother!" called Patsy.

There were two men in the Ulysses Room, and they paused in their conversation to glance up, but then returned to their talk. The Red Horse Room was empty.

"Mother!"

Suddenly, Henry ran out of the bedroom and through the Red Horse Room calling, "Patsy! I am glad you are home! You must run for the doctor right away!"

"What, Henry? I was just going to say *we* needed a doctor. Mrs. Brubaker . . ."

"Mother is going to have her baby," said Henry. "And Katherine says something may be wrong. They need help."

Mother! Mother is in danger! Fear froze Patsy in place.

"Go!" shouted Henry.

Patsy spun toward the door, grabbing Barbara by the hand. "We'll run as fast as we can!" she said.

The girls took off down Mulberry Street. Patsy and Barbara kept up with each other, hopping over puddles and dodging riders and wagons, holding their skirts to keep from tripping. Patsy's mind and heart were in a terrible whirl.

Mother is having her baby, and there is something wrong! And Mrs. Brubaker is on the floor. What if she is dying?

They traveled down High Street, passing the music shop and the printers. They passed Boxler's Milliner, where their friend Abby, who was sweeping the stoop, paused to call out to them. But the girls ran on by without speaking.

We have to hurry! God help us!

"Here!" said Barbara. They had come to the apothecary. Above the shop of medicines was Dr. Willard's home.

Oh, please, Patsy prayed. *He must be home.* They pushed through the door. A chime over the door tinkled.

"I'll be a moment!" the doctor called from the back room. "I am with someone now. Please take your time and have a look around."

But Patsy didn't wait. She went to the backroom door and stuck her head through. The doctor was leaning over a man in a short chair, tugging at a molar with a curved metal hook. The man's face was ashen and his wig was knocked askew. He clearly wished he was anywhere else at this moment.

"Young ladies," Dr. Willard demanded, "I told you I'd . . ."

"Dr. Willard, we need your help right away!" Patsy blurted out. "Please! My mother is having her baby."

"I do not deliver babies," said Dr. Willard, continuing to tug with the hook. "That is a midwife's responsibility."

"But she is in trouble," said Barbara. "Patsy's brother asks for you to come, please, sir. And our neighbor Mrs. Brubaker is lying on the floor, deathly ill, we think."

Dr. Willard's expression changed to shock. "I will come, certainly!" He turned back at the man in the chair and with a quick flick of his wrist, snapped the molar from the man's jaw. The man grunted and put his hand to his mouth. The doctor handed him a rag. "Here, wipe your mouth, sir; there are ladies present." The doctor whirled in a circle, snatched his hat from a wall peg, and jammed it onto his head. He picked up a leather bag and said, "We are on our way, ladies!"

They went out to the street. The doctor's stride was twice as long as the girls', and they scrambled to keep up. Patsy held on to her bonnet. Her heart pounded and her arms were flushed with cold fear. Her legs were weak beneath her, but she pushed them onward, running as fast as she could. "Sir!" she called after him. "Is there another doctor so both ladies can be attended?"

Dr. Willard said, "The closest doctor, Mr. Williams, has gone off to mend those brought down in the battles. I will try my best to offer aid to both these women, with God's help."

They reached the tavern. Nicholas was outside on the walk, wringing his hands and hopping back and forth on his feet. He shouted when he saw them on the road. "Hurry, Doctor! My mother needs your help!"

"But what about Mrs. Brubaker?" asked Barbara. "Who should get help first?"

The doctor hesitated as if uncertain, himself, as to who needed assistance most. Patsy's stomach was twisted with fear, but she suddenly remembered her mother's words.

Women have been having babies ever since the world was created. We must trust the Lord to take care of us. And Patsy knew her mother would think she'd made the right decision. Her mother was stronger and would not want harm to come to Mrs. Brubaker.

Patsy pointed first to Mrs. Brubaker's house and said, "As we must choose someone to go first, then choose Mrs. Brubaker. She might well be dying. Her door is locked and we couldn't get in."

The doctor glanced quickly between the tavern and Mrs. Brubaker's house. Patsy said, "Sir, quickly, or she might die!"

"Patsy!" Nicholas shouted.

"Patsy!" cried Barbara.

Mother, please hold on. Be safe. You said not to worry. Wait for the doctor just a bit longer.

"Help Mrs. Brubaker first!" said Patsy. She ran to her neighbor's house, with Dr. Willard and Barbara following. The doctor lifted a booted foot and slammed it against the door. The door cracked but did not give. He kicked again, this time so hard his tricornered hat flew off into the grass. The lock gave way and the door swung inward. The doctor went inside and knelt beside Mrs. Brubaker. Patsy and Barbara stood just outside the door, watching. He put his hand to her face and said, "She is alive, but barely. We must get her off the floor immediately." He looked over his shoulder. "Girls, help me with her."

Nicholas was at the door now, panting and crying. "Doctor, my mother needs you!"

"Presently, I promise," said the doctor.

Patsy and Barbara each took one of Mrs. Brubaker's arms. The doctor took her legs, and they carried her upstairs to a beautifully decorated bedroom. Patsy was surprised at how light the woman was. Mrs. Brubaker made a little noise in her throat, but her eyes didn't open.

She might truly die, Patsy thought. *God help her and help my mother!*

"She has a fever," the doctor told Patsy and Barbara as he went to an oaken stand and emptied the water from the porcelain pitcher into the bowl. "She needs her face washed down until she wakens. Will you do this while I check on your mother?"

Patsy nodded.

The doctor said, "I will do my best for them both. Please try not to fret." He smiled a little smile, then went downstairs.

As Barbara dipped a handkerchief into the

water in the bowl and wrung it out, Patsy went to the window and looked out. Nicholas had grabbed on to the doctor's arm and was hurrying him toward the tavern.

Mother, don't die. Mother, I love you! she thought. Suddenly she felt faint herself. She reached out and took hold of the window hangings. Her knees began to shake and give way. Beads of sweat broke out on her neck and hands.

But strong arms went around her, and Barbara said, "Patsy, it was your idea to come here, and you aren't going to leave me alone with this. Your mother is getting help. Now stand up!"

Patsy took a deep breath. She locked her knees beneath her and took the wet handkerchief that Barbara was holding out to her. She looked at Mrs. Brubaker. The woman, with her face slack, seemed very old and helpless. Patsy put the handkerchief on the woman's brow. She could feel the fever rise through the cool of the cloth. *How strange to be with this nasty woman, so close, and yet now to feel no fear. I only feel pity for her now,* Patsy thought. Softly Patsy said, "Mrs. Brubaker, wake up."

Barbara stood close by Patsy's elbow, her arms

behind her back as if she didn't know what to do or say.

"Mrs. Brubaker, this is your neighbor, Patsy Black. Please open your eyes and let me know you are all right."

Mrs. Brubaker didn't open her eyes and she didn't stir. Patsy pressed the cloth to the woman's forehead, cheeks, chin, and neck. Then Barbara dipped it once more into the bowl of water, and Patsy tried again.

As Patsy dabbed the woman's face, Barbara walked around the room, her arms crossed. She studied the beautiful paintings on the wall, the carpet, the animal figurines on the mantel above the fireplace. Then she looked at the floor beside the bed and said, "Oh, Patsy, look!"

"I can't," said Patsy. "Mrs. Brubaker needs me."

Barbara came over and took the handkerchief from Patsy's hand. "Then let me, and you look on the floor on the other side of the bed."

Patsy walked around and stopped. There, on the floor, was a small ragged wool blanket. The blanket was covered with black and white hairs. Beside the blanket was a blue china bowl half full of water. "The puppy sleeps here," she said.

Across the bed, Barbara nodded. "She's been caring for it, not abusing it."

"Where is it now, I wonder?"

"I don't know."

Then there was a yip, and the puppy raced into the bedroom. He hopped onto the bed and licked the old woman's face.

"She lets him run the house," said Barbara. "She must like him very much."

Patsy rubbed her elbows and looked back at the wool blanket. The elderly woman was certainly a lonely soul, but she took comfort in a yapping, smelly puppy, even allowing it into her own bedchamber.

"I hope your mother is doing better," Barbara said, breaking Patsy's thoughts. "I'm certain the doctor can help her."

Patsy felt her stomach churn painfully with renewed worry. "I hope you're right," she said softly.

9

There was a thumping downstairs in Mrs. Brubaker's house, and Patsy could hear footsteps running up the steps. Nicholas called, "Patsy, where are you?"

"In here," Patsy said. She and Barbara had taken turns over the last hour, trying to cool Mrs. Brubaker's fever with the cold, wet handkerchief. The woman had stirred several times, but had not opened her eyes or spoken. Patsy wondered if she would ever wake up, or if she was truly going to slip into death. That was how Patsy's grandmother, Dorcas Black, had died four years ago. It was so sad, because Patsy didn't get a chance to say anything of importance to her before she was gone. Patsy sometimes imagined how nice it would have been just to tell her one last time how much she loved her.

"Patsy!" Nicholas's face burst in through the doorway, his fingers grasping each side of the frame. Patsy's heart jumped when she saw that her younger brother was smiling. "Patsy, the baby has come!"

"Yes? And how is Mother?"

"She's all so much better, Patsy," said Nicholas. "We waited and waited in the Red Horse Room, but the doctor would not have Father, Henry, and me see Mother all this time. And what a long wait it was. Babies are stubborn, I believe, taking so much time to arrive."

Patsy gave the cloth to Barbara and sat heavily on one of Mrs. Brubaker's elegant chairs. She was drained of energy but very happy. "And Mother is fine?"

"She is, Patsy. We went in to see her and she is quite fine, smiling and laughing. The baby is a strange creature, though. All red and wrinkled and wiggly."

"Don't you want to know if you have a brother or sister?" asked Barbara.

Patsy chuckled wearily. "I suppose it's another boy, isn't it, Nicholas?"

Nicholas shook his head. "It's a girl. Dorcas Ellen Black."

"A girl! And named after Grandmother!" Patsy hopped up and went to Nicholas, pulling him into the room and taking him in a tight embrace before he could squirm away with a grunt.

There was another set of footsteps on the stairs just then, heavier, steadier. Dr. Willard came into the bedroom. He put his bag on the floor and said, "How is Mrs. Brubaker?"

"Her fever is down a little," said Barbara. "But she has said nothing and has not moved."

"You girls are very brave," said the doctor. "I am proud of you. You may go on now, and I will stay with Mrs. Brubaker. Nicholas has agreed to stay with me a bit, too, in the chance I need an errand run. Go, Miss Black, and see your new sister."

Patsy grabbed Barbara's hand and the two girls went back to the tavern.

"Mother?" Patsy tapped on the bedroom door while Barbara, her hands folded and her bottom lip drawn in between her teeth, stood directly behind. Sunlight was warm through the western window of the Red Horse Room, bathing the clean wooden floor in a soft glow. "Mother, may I come in?"

"Patsy, of course!" came the faint but happy answer.

Patsy opened the door. The window blinds were drawn, and the room was dark and warm. On the mantel, two candles burned. Another two were on the small window-side table, their flames dancing lightly. Patsy could see her mother's form in the bed. "May Barbara come in, too?"

"Certainly."

The two girls went to the bed and stood, side by side. Patsy put her hand out and touched her mother's cheek, and her mother smiled. "We have a girl," Mrs. Black said. "A beautiful little girl." She then pulled back the fold of a blanket, revealing a tiny head and a tiny crown of feathery blond hair.

"Oh, look, Barbara. She's like a little doll," whispered Patsy.

"She's terribly small," said Barbara. But then she said, "Oh, I'm sorry. I don't mean to sound unkind."

But Mrs. Black shook her head. "She is terribly

small, Barbara. But isn't she lovely? Her name is Dorcas."

"I'm glad," said Patsy. "Grandmother would have been very proud to have a namesake." She leaned over and kissed her mother and her new little sister.

This will be fun, Patsy thought. *I can dress her up in pretty clothes and teach her to stitch and read and serve a proper tea.*

But then Dorcas's tiny eyes opened, her mouth drew up, and she began to cry loudly. Patsy stepped back from the bed, her eyes widening. "She may be little, but she's very loud."

Both Barbara and Mrs. Black began to laugh, and then Patsy did, too.

The following days moved along, mostly thick with intense heat, although an occasional cool breeze took the edge off it all. Henry took Nicholas down to the Delaware River, where the boys liked to swim. Patsy thought it might be fun on occasion to be a boy and to play in the water, but this year she was too busy to wonder much about it. Mrs. Black and Dorcas stayed in the bedroom, and not only did Patsy have her usual chores, but she was responsible for taking food to her mother and washing the baby's clothes in a separate tub.

The doctor visited Black's Tavern three days after Dorcas's birth to make sure Mrs. Black was doing better. He reported that Mrs. Brubaker was also improving, and that she was awake and alert.

"And back to her independent thinking," he added, with a wink to Mr. Black. Patsy thought, *That means she is back to being sour. Perhaps it is time for the Daughters of Liberty to go ask for the puppy.*

But as the doctor gave a slight bow and turned to leave, he said to Patsy, "Oh, yes, Mrs. Brubaker has asked me to give you this." He pulled a folded note from his waistcoat and handed it to her.

Patsy took the note and thanked the man, then followed him outside. She sat on a bench to the side of the stoop and opened the note. *It's from Mrs. Brubaker,* she thought. *What does she want from me?*

Patsy read,

Dear Miss Black,
     Please accept this invitation to visit my home tomorrow afternoon at two o'clock in

my parlor. I would greatly appreciate your asking your friend to join us. We need to talk.

>Yours,
>Mrs. Josiah Brubaker

Patsy folded the letter. She looked out across the street to the cooper's shop. Two men stood before the shop's door, arguing and pointing furious fingers at each other. Patsy doubted they were arguing over the price of a wet barrel. They were probably arguing over the goings-on down at the State House.

But for Patsy, the greatest worry for the moment was the idea of visiting Mrs. Brubaker in her parlor when the woman was wide awake and back to her grumpiness. Surely this was not meant to be a friendly visit. "We need to talk," she had written. Patsy could only guess that there was more chastisement lying in wait.

Henry and Nicholas came down the tavern walk. Both had wet hair, and Nicholas was holding his shoes in his hand.

"You look bothered," said Nicholas as he passed her on the stoop. "Did someone put bitter herbs in your tea?"

Patsy shook her head.

"We had a grand swim, Henry and I," Nicholas said. "You should have seen us. We had a race with some boys from Second Street. We were more skilled than they, I can assure you."

"That's fine," said Patsy.

The boys went inside. Collecting her thoughts and her skirt, Patsy went back to the stable to tell Barbara about Mrs. Brubaker's invitation.

"I don't think I'll go," said Barbara. She was preparing to take Little Bit out for a ride. The pony was tacked in her bridle and a man's saddle. Barbara was checking the girth to make sure it wasn't loose, to prevent an embarrassing spill out on the road. "The note was written to you."

"But she said to bring my friend."

"She didn't say me. You have other friends. Maybe she meant Abby Boxler."

"No, no!" said Patsy. "Please come with me. Mother knows I have a note and will ask this evening about it. So I must go, regardless. I don't want to venture into that woman's house alone now that she's better, Barb."

Barbara led Little Bit to the mounting block, climbed up, then stepped into the stirrup. She eased herself into the saddle and gathered the reins. Her skirt was tucked ungracefully, allowing her to sit astraddle. Mrs. Black would have had a fit to see it. "Patsy," Barbara said, "it doesn't sound like fun."

"You're frightened. I thought you were a brave Daughter of Liberty!" Patsy put her hands on her hips and gave Barbara a stern look.

Barbara frowned. "I am brave."

"Then come with me."

"I don't want to."

"Now that she's better we can once again tell her we want the puppy back."

"I don't want to."

Mr. Layman came out into the paddock. "Hello, Miss Black. And what are you two arguing over this time?"

Patsy saw her chance. "Mr. Layman, Mrs. Brubaker has invited Barbara and me over to her house tomorrow."

Patsy could see the furious sparks in Barbara's hazel eyes as Mr. Layman said, "That's very kind of her. Barbara, you must go, certainly. This is a good time to speak with that woman in her own home and make final amends."

"I thought helping her when she was ill made amends," said Barbara.

"Don't be impudent," said Mr. Layman. "That was a kindness anyone should have offered a sick neighbor. Go with Patsy tomorrow and be a good girl. You'll be glad you did, and so will I."

Under her breath, Barbara said, "Yes, sir." Then she clucked to Little Bit and the pony trotted out through the open back gate and to the alleyway behind the tavern grounds. She didn't even say good-bye to Patsy.

"Good afternoon, Patsy," said Mr. Layman as he crossed the paddock and went out to Mr. Norris's blacksmith shop.

"Good afternoon," Patsy answered. Then she thought, *I hope Barbara's not too mad at me. But we are really in this together, like it or not!*

10

Patsy couldn't help but laugh. She had never seen Barbara so scrubbed and clean in her whole life. She was even cleaner than on the night of the dance, if that was possible.

"Look at you!" Patsy said as the two girls met on the walk in front of the tavern. "You look like a queen!" Barbara was wearing her yellow dress, but over her shoulders was a lace shawl Patsy had never seen, and on Barbara's head was perched a hat that was just a little bit too big. She even carried a lacy pink parasol. Clearly Mrs. Layman had found something she thought appropriate for her daughter to wear for visiting a real lady. Barbara looked like a duck out of water.

She wrinkled her nose and tugged at the bonnet ribbon at her neck.

"We shall not have to visit long, shall we, Patsy?" she said. "This is all your doing, and I won't be made to sit still in that woman's home for hours."

Patsy said, "We will make it as quick as manners allow."

"Manners!"

"Yes, we must show manners. And then we'll ask for the puppy."

Barbara shook her head, but then laughed a little. "Lead on," she said. "We do like to take turns getting each other into predicaments, don't we?"

It took four knocks on Mrs. Brubaker's new door before there was any sound in the hall. Patsy had to work hard to keep her anxious fingers from clutching the material of her skirt into a tight ball. The door opened. It felt to Patsy as if a nest of caterpillars was in her stomach.

Mrs. Brubaker stood there looking much as she always had, tall and stern and imposing. It was as though the woman had never been sick at all.

"Come in, ladies," she said without so much as a smile. She stepped back and gestured with her hand, and Patsy and Barbara went inside. It was so much different from the way it had been when Mrs. Brubaker was ill. Patsy felt too uncomfortable to look around at all. She felt she was being studied and criticized by the old woman.

Mrs. Brubaker turned her back on the girls and proceeded down the hallway. Patsy looked at Barbara and rolled her eyes nervously. Then the girls followed.

There was a sunny parlor in the back, overlooking the backyard. As in the other rooms of the house, the parlor held many expensive furnishings, paintings, and carpets. On the table in the middle of the room was a fine silver tea set. The cups were certainly imported. On a silver platter was an array of tea cakes. Mrs. Brubaker indicated with a nod that the girls were to sit. They did, side by side on chairs so tall their feet barely touched the floor. Mrs. Brubaker silently lifted the silver tea pot and poured tea into the cups.

I wonder if I'll have the courage to ask for the puppy, Patsy thought as she watched the aromatic steaming tea fill her cup. *I seem to be much braver when I'm at my own house.*

Mrs. Brubaker took a chair across the table from the girls. She held her cup daintily and sipped. Patsy and Barbara followed suit. Even though Patsy knew etiquette, she found herself feeling clumsy and awkward. She sipped and put her cup back into its saucer.

Mrs. Brubaker spoke. "You girls tracked quite a bit of dirt into my house the other day. You and the doctor certainly did not check your shoes when you came into my home."

Patsy swallowed the tea. Her toes began to dance inside her shoes. Why was Mrs. Brubaker so mean all the time?

"But," said the woman. She looked out the back window, then to Patsy and Barbara again. "I do not think I have ever so appreciated any dirt as I did that dirt."

Barbara coughed, then put her hand to her mouth in an attempt at manners. Patsy said, "Excuse me?"

Mrs. Brubaker wasn't exactly smiling, but for the first time Patsy had known her, she wasn't exactly frowning, either. She said, "I did not invite you girls to scold you. I asked you to come share tea with me so I could thank you properly for saving my life."

"Oh," said Barbara. "Well . . ." She stopped and looked wordlessly at Patsy.

Patsy found her voice. "You're welcome, Mrs. Brubaker."

"And I have a small token of appreciation," said the woman. "If you will kindly indulge me for a moment, I shall be right back." Mrs. Brubaker left the parlor.

Patsy took several sips of her tea. Barbara whispered, "A token? I can't believe my ears, Patsy. Mrs. Brubaker wants to give us something."

Mrs. Brubaker returned. She stopped in the doorway, holding the little black and white puppy. Like Barbara, the dog had never been so clean; his white and black spots practically gleamed. He had gained weight from eating well. His little black eyes shone like bits of coal.

"I believe you were after him in my garden," Mrs. Brubaker said. "And though I will never condone trespassing, and suggest you two never do such a thing again, I would like to return the dog to his rightful owners."

Barbara jumped to her feet and clapped her hands. "Yes, thank you!"

But Patsy remained seated, and she said, "No, thank you, Mrs. Brubaker."

Both Mrs. Brubaker and Barbara stared in shock at Patsy.

Patsy remembered the wool blanket on the floor beside Mrs. Brubaker's bed. She remembered the china bowl. This woman clearly loved the puppy as much as Patsy did, maybe even more. The woman was so lonely, she needed something to love and something that would love her back. To take the puppy away from his new home would be wrong.

"I'd like you to keep the dog," Patsy said. Out of the corner of her eye, she could see Barbara preparing to argue, but she continued. "I see that the puppy has a fine home here, and much more than we can offer at the tavern or the stable. I would feel much better if he made his home here."

Patsy saw something on the old woman's face that she had never thought possible. She saw surprise and a touch of softness. "Miss Black, I would not propose to keep something which does not belong to me," Mrs. Brubaker said.

"He belongs to you as much as to me," said Patsy. "I found him, a stray along the road. You found him, a stray in your beautiful garden. I think he likes you very much. He is wagging his tail so desperately hard it looks as though he'll flip upside down."

Mrs. Brubaker slowly lowered the puppy to the floor. He barked at her, hopped up and down a bit, then went exploring under the parlor table. Mrs. Brubaker frowned, but the frown this time wasn't one of anger. It seemed as if she was trying to keep from crying. She said, "My dear, you are being too kind."

"Not at all," said Patsy.

Mrs. Brubaker put a finger to her lips. "Would you consider sharing the puppy, then? We could take turns watching out for him. He might be happier with more mistresses and two households."

Patsy grinned. "Yes, that would be fine! Let's share the puppy!"

At last Barbara spoke up. "I think sharing is the best way." Patsy looked at her friend and gave her a wink.

The rest of the tea was more pleasant than Patsy could have imagined. Even though Mrs. Brubaker's face returned to its usual comfortable scowl and her voice retained its gruffness, her words were nothing but kind. After nearly an hour of visiting, Mrs. Brubaker escorted the girls to the front door and said, "As weary as I am, still recovering from that dreadful day, I fear I must venture out. There is a bonnet I ordered from Boxler's Milliner quite some time ago and they needn't wait any longer for recompense."

"We will be happy to go for you," said Barbara. "It will be our pleasure."

"And we will take the puppy with us so he can stretch his legs," added Patsy.

Mrs. Brubaker was appreciative and gave the girls a pouch full of shillings for the purchase of the hat. As the puppy bounded out to the sunny walkway, barking and jumping, Patsy said, "What do you call the puppy, Mrs. Brubaker? Barbara and I had never come to agreement on a name."

"I just call him George."

"Why is that?"

"He's an adventurer," said Mrs. Brubaker. "He has spirit, like another George of which I know. Not the king, but another one. A patriot. A leader of our army."

The girls went next door and told Katherine that they would be gone for a short while. Katherine said not to worry, she was looking in on Mrs. Black and things were well in hand at the tavern.

The walk to Boxler's Milliner took the girls down long stretches of road and through the middle of the city's central marketplace on High Street. George bounced along, sometimes in front of the girls, sometimes behind. The market consisted of open buildings in the middle of the street, stretching all the way from First to Fourth Streets. Here citizens swarmed, purchasing all kinds of foods such as vegetables, eggs, fish, cheese, butter, beef, pork, and opossum, bear, and raccoon meat. Conestoga wagons painted in bright red and blue were parked at market side. Farm families scrambled back and forth from the wagons to the open buildings with their produce. Patsy remembered the marketplace as being cheerful and lively when she was younger. But with the war around and about, if not directly in Philadelphia, the tone was businesslike and much more somber. There was just as much talk, and indeed occasional laughter, but many of the words were draped in seriousness and tension.

Just before entering the marketplace, Patsy and Barbara passed the stocks and pillory. Both were occupied by prisoners. At the stocks a man sat on a narrow strip of wood with his feet secured in the wooden frame out before him. At the pillory a man stood with his head and hands locked into a similar frame. Neither man looked very happy or comfortable. On both men's faces were traces of rotten drying tomato. Boys who visited the marketplace often enjoyed taunting the prisoners by hurling rotten fruits and vegetables. Patsy could never imagine doing such a thing. In fact, she found it unsettling to look the prisoners in the eye as she passed. How she would hate it if her punishment of sitting in the straight-backed chair was moved to the street for the enjoyment of her neighbors.

"Come on, Patsy!" called Barbara. Patsy noticed that her thoughts had slowed her step. Barbara was already well ahead, moving through a market building. Patsy ran to catch up.

They turned onto a small side road to cross over to the milliner's shop. The stretch was dirty, rutted, and spotted with garbage tossed out by shopkeepers. A feral pig rooting in some rotten vegetables squealed and ran off into the shadows behind a hedgerow. Barbara suddenly stopped. "I forgot to give you something!" she said.

Patsy stopped. George, who had been keeping up, ran ahead several yards, then turned back and looked at the girls as if to say, "We have places to go. Come on!" But Barbara proceeded to pull off her left shoe and take something from it. Then she stuck the shoe back on.

"What's that?" Patsy asked.

"A coded message," Barbara said with a huge grin. "A really important message this time, from one Daughter of Liberty to another."

"A coded message about what?"

"It wouldn't be much of a code or much of a message if I told you."

Patsy looked at the folded piece of paper that was thrust in her direction. "But it's been in your shoe all day."

"What's wrong with that?"

Patsy's nose wrinkled. "Just shake it out a little then and I'll take it." *Playing Daughters of Liberty is fun,* she thought. *But wouldn't it be something if we really could make a difference, like the Sons of Liberty did? If we could do something more than just trying to rescue puppies and passing notes back and forth to each other.*

Barbara fanned the small piece of paper back and forth, laughing at her friend's pinched face, and then Patsy took it reluctantly. But a new shadow fell across the ruts of the narrow road. Both Patsy and Barbara looked up, and the puppy stopped playing to stare.

It wasn't something unusual, only a man riding his horse. But the man seemed nervous. His chestnut horse, clearly a spirited animal by its high prancing and side stepping, was reined in tightly. The man had his tricornered hat pulled way down on his face, as if he were afraid someone might recognize him. A haversack on a leather strap was slung over his shoulder. His chin was tucked down against his chest and he stared quickly at the girls, then away.

Patsy's first thought was that the man was a thief, and he was hiding on the street. But then she decided that that was a silly notion. One could never judge another from appearances. Look at Mrs. Brubaker. Who could have known that under the scowl was a nice lady?

The man rode between Barbara and Patsy. The horse snorted and tried to break into a trot, but the man would have nothing of it. His wrists flexed, drawing the reins in even more tightly.

Suddenly George decided it was right to nip the horse on the ankle. Patsy shouted out as the dog lunged forward, but it did no good. The horse reared, tossing its head wildly and jerking the reins from the grasp of the mysterious man. The man was dumped backward off the horse, striking the ground. His head bounced once, and he lay still. The horse bolted and disappeared around the corner at the end of the street.

"Oh!" Barbara shouted to George. "What have you done, you terrible rascal!"

"The man is hurt," said Patsy. "Go call for help. I'll stay with him!"

As George stood sniffing at the unconscious man, Patsy knelt beside him, tentatively touching his hand and feeling that he was still very much alive. Barbara whirled about and ran out of the narrow street. She shouted to the passersby, "Quickly, please! A man has fallen from his horse and I fear is severely hurt!"

Two men who had been strolling side by side immediately followed Barbara back to the place where the man lay. They tried to speak to him, to shake and wake him, and with a little prodding, he did at last open his eyes slightly. Then the men lifted him and carried him off.

Patsy and Barbara watched them go. Then Patsy turned a stern face toward the puppy. "You will be tied up! I shall not have you doing such things to people. The man could have been killed. It is with great luck he was not." She scooped the puppy up and held him tightly. "You will be carried until we arrive at the milliner's. Then I shall ask for a rope for you, to tie about your neck on our way home."

Boxler's Milliner was not far, and it took just a few minutes to arrive. Mrs. Layman was inside, happy to see the girls. Abby was there, too, helping Mrs. Layman make a window display of new hats. Abby was a pretty girl with dark hair and eyes. She was good at needlework and could play a harpsichord.

"Oh, let me see!" Abby exclaimed as Patsy entered the shop, holding George. "What a sweet dog!"

But Patsy shook her head. "Not so sweet. He had a man tossed from his horse. I dare say this dog has more energy than I know how to handle."

"A man was hurt?" asked Mrs. Layman. She came around the counter and took Barbara by the shoulders. "I'm sorry to hear that. And you, are you hurt?"

"No," said Barbara.

"The puppy should be left at home," said Mrs. Layman.

"From now on, we will," said Patsy. "He belongs to Mrs. Brubaker now, at least for half the time. She will teach him manners, I'm certain."

Abby took George and buried her face in his wriggly body. "I think he is precious. Any puppy likes to chase a horse. The man must have been a poor rider to have been tossed so easily."

Mrs. Boxler appeared from the back room. She was a large woman with a happy smile and a mad spray of red hair beneath her mobcap. "Good afternoon, ladies! And to what do I attribute a visit?"

"We are on an errand from Mrs. Brubaker," said Patsy. "To collect a hat she ordered."

"Hmm," said Mrs. Boxler. "You are on speaking terms now with Mrs. Brubaker?"

"She's nicer than we thought," said Barbara. "We had tea and cakes at her home just a short while ago."

"I'm glad to hear it," said Mrs. Boxler. "With all the fighting these days, it's nice to know there is some peacemaking going on as well. And how is your lovely mother and the new little Dorcas?"

"In excellent health, thank you," said Patsy.

"And now for Mrs. Brubaker's hat," said Mrs. Boxler. From a wall shelf behind her she lifted a large straw hat decorated with green satin bows. "Here! And a finer piece of work you'd never find from England. Take care you don't muss it on the way home."

"Oh, one more thing," said Barbara. "Have you any rope?"

A minute later the girls were back out on the street. Barbara carried the hat while Patsy tugged on George's new leash. The puppy was at first resistant, then gave in to being led. Patsy stopped at the street corner. She had been holding a new secret long enough. "We aren't far from the State House," she said.

Barbara said, "I know that. What does it matter?"

"I think we should go. As Daughters of Liberty."

"What are you saying? You make no sense. The Congress is meeting. They won't have two girls hanging about."

But Patsy could barely keep the excitement from her voice. Her eyebrows danced up and down. "I said nothing until now because I only wanted it between me and you, not my mother or Abby or Mrs. Boxler. I found a note!"

"A note?"

"In the man's haversack. When he fell from the horse, his sack popped open and I found a note.

It seems to be of true importance, Barb. I had just a second to look at it, but I recognized the words *army* and *river*. I quickly snatched it up and hid it in my . . ."

"Your shoe! You learned that from me!"

"No, silly, not my shoe." Patsy pulled a small crumpled piece of paper from the lace at the bottom of her sleeve. "Let's read it. See if we don't think it is something the Daughters of Liberty should take with haste to the Congress at the State House."

Patsy handed the end of the rope to Barbara and flattened the note. She was surprised to find her fingers trembling a bit. Was this truly something of importance?

The note said:

A few of the army will arrive at the river by the 29th. Send word to K. G. F. immediately to meet at F. T. Will await orders.

"This makes no sense," said Barbara.

"Not to us," said Patsy. "But to the men of Congress it could mean a great deal. Barb, I believe the man George knocked off his horse is a patriot secretly carrying a message intended for

Congress. This message must get to the State House right away!"

"But Mrs. Brubaker is waiting for her bonnet."

"Are you afraid? A Daughter of Liberty afraid to do an important chore?"

"No!" said Barbara. "Let's go to the State House."

Patsy and Barbara linked arms and hastened to Chestnut Street. George, seeming to pick up on the excitement, tried to run ahead, tugging strongly on his rope.

The State House was an impressive yet plain brick building, built in 1735. The center section was two stories high with a belfry, and the west and east wings of a single story. In the belfry, a bell known as the "American Bell" was rung on many important occasions. A large grassy lawn stretched out before it. In this building lectures were given and dances were held, and important men gathered in this place for meetings of all sorts.

And on this afternoon, the Continental Congress was using the State House for its business. From listening to the talks at Black's Tavern, Patsy knew the men were wrestling with the idea of declaring independence from the king of England.

Patsy, Barbara, and George crossed the grassy yard. Patsy felt a sudden shiver of fear. Serious talks and debates were going on at the State House. What right did she and Barbara have to include these men in their Daughters of Liberty game?

But it isn't a game anymore, she reminded herself. The note she had contained an important message for someone. Patsy went right up to the front door and knocked loudly. In a moment, a young man opened it and gazed down at the girls.

"How may I help you ladies?" he asked.

"We have a message," said Patsy. "We found it on a fallen rider. We believe it is something the Congress should have."

"It must be read right away," Barbara added.

The man nodded, but Patsy could see his smile. It was as though he thought they were indeed playing and he was humoring them. "We thank you, ladies," he said as Patsy gave him the note. "And a good day to you."

The door closed. Barbara and Patsy looked at each other.

"That's it?" asked Barbara. "Thank you and

good day? After all we did?" Her shoulders drooped. Clearly she had wanted to be a heroine.

"We took the note to them," said Patsy. "Now they must read it and determine its worth. We did what we were supposed to do. Now we'll take the bonnet to Mrs. Brubaker."

Slowly the girls crossed back over the yard. Even George walked with less enthusiasm, as if he, too, were disappointed.

But then there was a shout from the State House door. Patsy and Barbara turned around, and the young man was trotting across the grass toward them.

"Ladies!" he said. "Wait just a moment. I took the note inside, and indeed it was a message we needed to see. This man who had the note. Where is he now?"

"I'm not certain," said Patsy. "He was taken off to a doctor, I believe."

The man stooped down to look both girls in the eye. "You have brought us a note from a spy," he said. "The man was carrying a message about the movement of one of the king's regiments. Thank you again for your help. And great help it certainly was!" He stood and went back into the building.

Neither Patsy nor Barbara said anything for a moment. Then Barbara burst into giggles. "We are truly Daughters of Liberty!" she said.

Patsy joined in the laughter. "Yes! We are brave after all, and we did something to help the patriots' cause!"

Even George barked happily.

Barbara put Mrs. Brubaker's hat on her head. The girls strolled up the road on their way to the tavern.

After a few minutes of silence, Barbara said, "Have you read the note I gave you? It is in our code, of course!"

"I don't have it anymore. I traded it for the man's note. I put it into his haversack. After the troubles we've had with trespassing and ruining gardens, I didn't want to be accused of stealing as well. And so I didn't steal. I traded!"

Barbara laughed. "Oh, no matter. It wasn't a serious matter. I buried some treasure in the paddock, is all. I dug a hole and put in some scraps from Mr. Norris's blacksmith shop. Not very exciting compared to what happened today. From now on, I think the Daughters of Liberty will be a lot more than just a game."

Patsy said, "I think so, too!"

They began to skip side by side, arms linked. Mrs. Brubaker's hat bobbed on top of Barbara's head like a boat on the Delaware River. Patsy thought, *I wonder what new adventures the Daughters of Liberty will have? We'll keep our eyes and ears open and see how we can help.*

George barked happily and ran hard on his little spotted legs, keeping up.

About the Author

Elizabeth Massie was born, raised, and still lives in the Shenandoah Valley of Virginia. As a kid she loved horses, reading *Happy Hollister* books, watching the Monkees on TV, making scary tape recordings, and adding new roads, rivers, and houses to the room-sized map she and her sisters worked on in their basement for over a year. Ms. Massie taught science for nineteen years in grades five, six, and seven, and now enjoys writing full-time for adults and younger readers. She is the mother of two children—Erin, age 20, and Brian, age 18—and in her spare time loves traveling, reading, camping, hiking, and horseback riding and coming up with new writing projects with her sister, Barbara Spilman Lawson.

DAUGHTERS *of* LIBERTY

INDEPENDENCE DAY 1776

It all started with the Daughters of Liberty
and their adventures in Philadelphia....

PATSY'S DISCOVERY

PATSY AND THE DECLARATION
(Coming in mid-July 1997)

BARBARA'S ESCAPE
(Coming in mid-August 1997)

By Elizabeth Massie

 A MINSTREL® BOOK
Published by Pocket Books   1337-01